Praise for *The Peleg Chronicles*

Blue Ribbon Award for Best Book 2010-2011
— The Old Schoolhouse Magazine

"Like gnarled roots of an old tree, these stories twist and turn, entangling you in anticipation to see how they all unwind …
The story follows the heroic adventures of a handful of God-fearing men and children. These often funny and endearing characters show us what can be accomplished when you learn to overcome your fears and walk in faith …
The books read like fantasy novels, yet without magic spells, wands, and flying broomsticks. Instead, Scripture and prayer are revealed as the powerful tools needed to overcome the works of those who obey the evil one; to offer hope to our heroes in desperate times; and to give them boldness to share their faith along the way. God's redemptive power is also plainly evident when even a sworn enemy can turn to the one true God …
A thrilling cliffhanger ends each story so be sure to read them in order. I can't wait to find out what happens in the next one.
Maybe these "magic-free" character-building, God-honoring novels will start a new trend … I hope so!"

— Nigel Andreola, *Christian Book Distributors*

"Great book! I would like the book to be about 500 pages; no, 600 pages. The doctrines and examples are powerful. Can you do a new series about the Giants? Maybe a short story? How about Fergus' training from a youth? Thiery's memorization days with Oded? Back story, side story, or continuing story! Maybe even a short play by Gettlefinger? Your stories are a delight to my family. Your messages strengthen our faith. Your doctrines strengthen our resolve to live by God's word alone. Sola Scriptura. May God be prais

— Peter Rowell, father of

"I asked my daughter what she like so much about this book and she said "because there's no blank space. I mean, there's not any space where nothing's happening. There's always something important happening". I have read it and can say the same thing. There is excitement with every sentence. You won't want to put the book down, and when you come to the end … you're going to want more! It's refreshing to read such a wonderful book."

— **Mona Lisa,** *www.happilyhomeschooling.com*

"I believe this series is the answer to many parent's prayers."

— **Lauren,** *mother of 4*

"I completely and utterly love this book! … I loved everything about the book, especially Horatio. I can't wait for more!"

— **Courtney,** *age 16*

"At first, I was a bit hesitant because I am not a giant and dragon type of girl. However, I found myself anxious each night to indulge in the lives of these notorious characters. Such an uplifting reading experience involving courage and faith … a read aloud at its best."

— **Mom of six**

"Both of my sons, ages 15 and 16, greatly enjoyed the book. The real surprise is that I loved it too! This is not the type of story I would normally read for enjoyment."

— **Lorie**, *homeschool mom*

"This book gets not only approval but a standing ovation. Do not be mistaken and think this book will also be devoid of adventure, thrills, fun and challenging thoughts. Foundlings not only gives you a ride that combats any roller coaster it gives you a true sense of heroism and family discussions that center on the glory of God's creation and Word. Think your kid is not interested in the Bible or Christian books? This book will change both your minds."

— **Richele,** *Under the Golden Apple Tree*

Matthew Christian Harding

LORESMEN

Zoe and Sozo Publishing
3034 Millers Landing Rd.
Gloucester, Virginia 23061

www.MatthewChristianHarding.com

Cover Design by Zoe and Sozo Publishing

All scripture references are from the King James Version of the Bible.

ISBN 978-0-9823484-2-0

For my grandparents,

Grandma and Grandpa Harding
Grandma and Grandpa Gunderson
Grandma and Grandpa Gallup
Grandma and Grandpa Pickerign

For my parents,

Mom and Dad
Mom Debby
Mom Julie
Dad Ross
Dad Doug

For my siblings,

Heather
Josh
Tiara
Keelin

Table of Contents

LIST OF CHARACTERS

Thiery- *foundling, aspiring ranger and beast-master.*
Suzie- *foundling, adopted sister of Thiery.*

Oded- *son of a giant, slow witted, gentle but capable warrior; ranger and beast-master; guardian of Thiery and Suzie.*
Ubaldo- *Oded's deaf twin; ranger and beast-master.*

Count Rosencross- *hungry for power and personal glory, yet an awakening conscience plagues him.*
The Priest- *the Count's personal Dragon Priest; tried to sacrifice his son, Thiery, to his false god.*

The Chronicler- *Master of the Citadel; over 200 years old, lived in Babel before the dispersion.*
Diego Dandolo- *the Chronicler's assistant, former sneak.*

Staffsmitten- *honorary non-dwarf member of the Dwarven Brotherhood, lesser gate-keeper, naturalist, friend of Gimcrack.*
Gimcrack- *map-maker, inventor, dwarf; scared of water... Dragon Priests... boats... the dark... graveyards... and maybe a few other things.*
Cnutfoot- *Prince of the Dwarven Brotherhood, son of Lord Redwald.*

Lord Tostig- *drugged and captured with his men, by Rosencross; saved from slavery by Thiery and a dragon attack.*
Blagger- *one of Lord Tostig's warriors.*

Aramis- *captain of a band of mercenaries; McDougal's childhood torturer.*

Lord McDougal- *paragon of chivalry, awkward hero, landless lord.*
Fergus Leatherhead- *faithful shield-bearer to Lord McDougal, ranger.*
Igi Forkbeard- *ex-slaver of Count Rosencross, joined McDougal's party.*
Mercy- *niece of the King, rescued from the Priests of Bachus.*

Gettlefinger- *aka Grimesby, aka Craven Dregs; head of Hradcanny's thespian society.*

King Strongbow- *warrior King, consumed with a drive to please the masses, unstable mind.*
Queen Miriam- *sad, lonely, and fearful that the king will slip into insanity.*
Princess Catrina- *seeker of self, pleasure, and the false gods.*

Witch Esla- *false prophetess seeking the demise of Lord McDougal.*
Squilby- *one of the masters of the Citadel, dwarf, delights in wickedness.*

Pip- *young sneak, quick, eager and loyal.*
Percival- *(Pup) 5 year old younger brother of Pip; beggar.*

Lunace, Ogre, and Goblin- *superstitious and greedy giants; captured Igi Forkbeard in book one.*

Horatio- *Thiery's white wolf, giant variety.*
Woolly- *Ubaldo's woolly mammoth.*
Birdie- *Oded's talking bird.*
Griz- *Oded's grizzly bear.*
Mamma- *matriarch of the badger clan, studied by Staffsmitten.*

Prologue

The rendering of this tale flings itself forward not unlike the homing pigeon sent forth with its missive. It leaps into the sky circling.

Which way will it go?

This is not known to those who observe from below — excepting, perhaps, by the one who set it free to commence its flight.

Suddenly it bursts in a straight line, one which will take it great distances if need be, and with tenacious speed. It wants to come home, and the tale wants its proper end. For these birds love their mates, and dote upon their young. Yes, it wants to come home, and the tale wants its proper end.

Yet there are enemies of the pigeon: rats, weasels, mice, and hawks. They crave to bring it down, to slay it while it sleeps or soars. And the pigeon cannot fight, but flee only.

Many a rat creeps.

The beady eyes of Elvodug and Flemup search after Suzie.

Weasels slither and lurk.

The witch Esla speaks words that lie and flatter in the ears of King Strongbow. The Dragon Priest pulls tight the net of evil around his prey. Rosencross struggles in the cords thereof, and only One can cut him free.

Thiery also, he strives to understand; he walks with his Lord and seeks to find Oded and the others; a boy of prayer with always a glance over his shoulder; a quick look to the shadows and a wary eye upon those he meets.

Do not forget Lunace, Goblin, and Ogre, the giants who wish to rend and kill. Winning battles is what they enjoy most; they are men of violence who stand at the barred gates of the arena, eager to pour forth their might upon the heroes of Hradcanny.

What is at stake? The very life of Lady Mercy; sought by the followers of Bacchus and the Queen of Heaven.

And what of Master Squilby? With his flying creature to carry him, he may strike from the air or slink upon the ground, with Sneeks, Death-Hound Riders, and hyenae at his command.

The tale will certainly come to an end, but shall the pigeon find its home? Will it fly straight and true? Come and see.

The Letter

The Chronicler sat at his desk, empty but for his bell and scroll-weights holding back the corners of a large pigeon-parchment. It was a note from Lord Tostig describing the trial of Igi Forkbeard. Tostig was always detailed with his narrations; one seemingly unimportant revelation had astounded the Chronicler, yes, and it had pleased him very much; a name had been revealed — Thiery. It seemed that he was not dead after all, though it was unclear exactly where he might be found. Both Tostig and Igi had seen him, in fact the boy had saved them from a dragon. The Chronicler felt great pleasure at the thought.

There was a faraway look in his eyes as he mused over this very good news.

So now there were two to find. He had called all the guardians that still lived to the task of finding Suzie, and now he would set them on the trail of Thiery as well. He had even sent for Redhand — not exactly a godly man or even a good man, in fact it had not been an easy decision, but there it was, and no one could stay hidden from Redhand for long.

His thoughts came back to Suzie, and he wondered how it was that he had not known of her sooner. He had forgotten to question Oded about the matter; after the games he would learn her story. In any event, he would make sure she was taken care of; what was one more to add to his will? He took out pen and scroll. He paused and thought some more of the little girl. Maybe he could dandy her upon his knee yet, hug her close, and maybe she would one day even call him her hero.

The Chronicler smiled and spoke to himself, "You are becoming quite a tender-heart in your old age. But I suppose reading the letter again would not be remiss." It was getting difficult to get work done, when always he felt the beckoning call of the letter. More and more of late he felt bound to its contents.

He reached under his desk and pressed the hidden catch. A click. A drawer rolled forward. The Chronicler pulled out the contents and began to read.

My dear Grandfather,

I hope you do not mind that I call you by such an intimate name. I heard my Great Uncle Lestrath call you by it many times when I was growing. And perhaps you do not recall, but once when I was a little girl, we came to visit the court, and as you were passing by with an immense book in your arms, you paused, looked down at my pitiful tears — for I was crying over some childish thing which I cannot recall — and you took a moment to dandy me upon your knee.

I knew who you were at once. I called you grandfather then. You seemed confused and even uncomfortable. So I told you who I was. You smiled and said that you would always like for me to call you thus.

That was the only time I ever saw you. But I felt so very safe in your arms. While you will surely struggle to place me in your family tree, and perhaps not recollect that day at all, you have been close to me in that I have read your writings which have stirred my soul to follow God, and I have called you grandfather in my prayers and dreams ever since; so you see, it comes quite naturally to me, to call you by such a title. I hope my claim to it still meets with your acceptance. If I must place all the greats that you deserve before grandfather, I'm afraid you will feel so very old and I will feel so very far.

I write you now, many years from that happy day, as the Countess of Bannockburn*, and one in dire need of your assistance. Circumstances are such that I must ask you not to write back, or if you do, that your message comes to me quite secretly. I have prepared this packet of letters in hope that I might find a way to get them to you without my husband, the Count* Rosencross *of* Bannockburn*, or any of his people, made the wiser to their existence or of my delivering them to you. I only await God's timing to make a way for it to happen.*

Please do not judge my husband too harshly. If what I suspect is true then he has done great wickedness, and yet I still hope for him. I love him still and do not wish for any to perish in Hell*, to where it is I so fear he might go.*

There was a time when he was a defender of the faith, at least I was convinced that he was, but I'm afraid that the cares of this world have overcharged his heart; the pride of life has conquered his conscience, and he fears the loss of what he has, while he yet covets that which he has not.

It all began when an old fisherman came to our port village speaking of the days not long before when the ocean came close to our castle — almost to its very walls. For now it is quite far, yet still visible from the parapets. He said the gods of the north were drawing it into their cheeks, and then through the coldness of their hearts they were spitting it back out in the form of the ice mountains, which creep ever closer to crush us; that is, if the gods are not appeased.

My husband led the expedition himself to find out what truth might be in these words. He had not gone far from our own lands when he saw the ashy ice wall across the horizon.

Seven years earlier, when he had last traveled that way, there had been no walls of ice. Yet there they stood. His own heart began to turn cold towards the God of Noah, and then he searched for a god who could save him from the invading ice.

And so he journeyed by ship to faraway lands. The days after his return, he could be found staring off to sea. The children were eager to see their father; we cried to him, ever calling him to stay with us, to come back to the true God, to right, to love. Belfry, Clovis, and Arsuf, that were their names, the sons of Count Rosencross of Bannockburn, my beautiful boys, ever calling their father to come home.

One day he came from across the seas with an evil aboard his ship, worse than any he had brought before; two red robed priests of the Dragon Cult. I shuddered whenever they were near, but at least my husband was home. Then the six-fingered giants of the north — their own homeland shrinking from the encroaching ice — struck a blow at us. That was when my oldest, Belfry, still only a boy, fell from a battlement.

My husband stood before me that night, after the giants had been driven back in defeat, to tell me of my son. The Count was ghastly white, he shook violently, and upon his hands he wore white gloves - gloves which would never again be removed in my presence. One of the servants told me of whisperings that Belfry's death had not been an accident. On the morrow, my servant went missing.

Next, it was a neighboring lord, growing in strength, who threatened our border. The details do not matter, but soon after, Clovis and Arsuf too, were laid in the grave. My dear sweet boys.

The priests of the Dragon were ever at my husband's side, his favored counselors, and dark was that counsel. With care, I uncovered the Dragon Priests' ways; that they followed the sun god, Marduk, and that while they do not cause young ones to pass through the fire, they do practice sacrifices in secret; so that even their intended victims are not aware of their danger. There is much more that I have seen and heard, but I will not put it to pen; suffice it to say that I believe these horrid practices account for the suspect manner and timing of my darling ones departing.

Moreover, I think that I might soon be joining them; looking forward to our reunion almost as much as I look forward to seeing our King of Kings — if it were not for the one I leave behind. For you see, soon after the loss of Clovis and Arsuf, I found myself with child, and my foreboding was great indeed. Hourly were my prayers that God would keep this one safe from harm. At first I was able to keep the slight growing of my middle a secret, and then the providence of God sent the Count away on a very long journey.

I withdrew to quiet mourning within a tower of the castle, hiding myself away from all but a few trusted servants. No one thought it a strange thing for their Countess to shut herself so far from the world, since they believed the world had dealt me blows from which anyone would need time to recover.

It has been difficult, but God's grace has been more than sufficient for my needs. Truly I was joyful in the day of prosperity, and in the day of adversity I considered: God also hath set the one over against the other, to the end that man should find nothing after Him. Perhaps my silver had become like dross, and I was in need of refining; and I was tried as gold is tried so that I would call on His name, and He would hear me.

I called upon Him and I have found His peace which passeth all understanding. I shall not draw back no matter my earthly lot, but I will believe to the saving of the soul.

The boy was born healthy and strong while his father was still away. He is to be raised nearby, but alas not by me, for I fear what the priests will do with him, and I fear to what degree his father is to blame. I slip away to hold him whenever it seems safe enough to do so, while he is yet still a babe, but the Count has returned, and with many more of those cursed priests. My husband is a very different man from what he was, and now I grow weaker every day - for what reason I do not know. I think our God shall call me home soon.

The priests are everywhere and I do not know whom to trust. I am even afraid to name my son, lest while I sleep I should call out to him and somehow give away my secret.

Please, I beg you, my Grandfather, send guardians to keep my son safe, ones who love our God and will train the boy, without compromise, in His ways. It is his soul that I wish to protect, much more than the body, which I know well is but a temporary home. But eternity, dear Grandfather, that is where I pray and hope to see him. Perchance, when he is old enough, you could even take him into your keeping.

I know I ask much of you, from a granddaughter with so many greats between you and her, and only one very small moment when you hugged me close and became my hero. To you I must seem a stranger. But I beseech you as kin, as a woman and mother in need, and as a follower of the one true God, please help. Please do not leave my son without one who is faithful to stand by him as he grows.

Woe to him that is alone when he falleth; for he hath not another to help him up, and if one prevail against him, two shall withstand him, and a threefold cord is not quickly broken. Oh, that God would be forever the binding cord of my son's life.

To the glory of our God and King!
With hope in my heart I do write,
Countess Johanna of Bannockburn

The Chronicler sighed and spoke aloud. "It is a good letter, Johanna. My soul is stirred when I think of how God raised up such a lovely young lady as you were. How many more shall He raise up, like you, down through the centuries, and what privileged men shall marry them, and what privileged children shall be born to them, if they show even an inkling of your faith."

The Arena

Fergus Leatherhead stood at the portcullis. Blagger was at his side. They looked grimly out at the arena floor. Igi Forkbeard was to their left, behind another gate. He looked recovered, but Fergus could not help but be concerned that Igi's freshly healed wounds would not withstand the rigors of battle.

To their right stood the mighty twins, Oded and Ubaldo; they both held massive war hammers that looked more like large wooden chests than weapons; formidable indeed when viewed as something intended for bashing shield and armor. The twins looked intimidating, at least until Oded appeared to forget the grave reasons for their assembling.

Oded was trying to get someone's attention. Was he waving to Igi? If so it was an embarrassing spectacle to behold. Oded was blushing, shrugging his shoulders, twisting this way and that, waving a timid hand, then covering his face, and then waving again. His brutal war hammer forgotten at his side. All forty thousand of the spectators were hushed and expectant; but soon there was a swelling titter from the tiered balconies above as some of the onlookers began to take note of Oded's singular behavior.

What was he doing? Fergus looked again towards Igi, but he did not move, wave, or smile. Then he looked up to the king's royal platform where he at once perceived the inspiration behind Oded's antics. It was Lady Mercy. Delicate and noble in appearance, encircled by priests of Bacchus, she looked neither alarmed nor embarrassed. She smiled and waved at Oded in return.

Ubaldo was now signing something to Oded which immediately brought an end to his childish display. It was Fergus's lot to be allied with warriors uncouth in the ways of manly presentation. It struck him that maybe he could make up for his old thoughts, habits and feelings, which Lord McDougal had frequently provoked, by being especially forbearing with Oded. He would try. He thought it likely that God was trying to teach him something and he had better humble himself before it, or God might just bestow on Fergus someone like Mr. Gettlefinger as a companion in arms. He shuddered at the thought.

There was one gate left, directly across the arena floor from where Fergus and Blagger stood. Behind those black bars were the three giants, Lunace, Ogre, and Goblin. By the manner in which they were pointing and leering at Fergus, he guessed they remembered him.

"Why do you think they're pointing at us like that?" Blagger asked.

"I was part of a ruse," Fergus answered, "that cheated them of Igi Forkbeard's life, and I think they're glad for the chance to get even."

"Aye, they do look mighty pleased. My father used to say, 'Never fight a giant if you can help it. The strength behind their sword arm, will, with one stroke, break through your shield, then the arm that holds it, then the helmet upon your head, then the harebrained head that thought to stand up against a giant in the first place, and the blade will not rest 'til it hits the ground and splits you in two.' He had a way with words, my father did, and I always thought it good advice.

"But my sweet father knew not that I'd have to make a choice like this. I'm sure he'd never have spoken to me again if I'd turned my back on a friend in need or worse yet, if I didn't joyfully receive a blow in defense of a lady, even certain death at the hands of a giant."

"Hardly certain," Fergus said. "Oded and Ubaldo approach their size."

"I thought them big once, until I saw them and those giants at the same time." Blagger shrugged his shoulders. "This is a nasty business it is."

Fergus knew the difficulties with fighting men twice your size, and against weapons double the weight and length of your own. Once again he would be fighting for the Lady Mercy, but this time more than his honor and his life were at stake. The Bacchus Priests already hovered about their prey, anticipating the sinister conclusion their god required.

Fergus was growing annoyed. "We at least out number them."

Blagger continued, "Do you know that I think I can read the thoughts of the crowd? It is written upon their faces clear enough."

"And what do you see there, Blagger?"

"I see doubt that we five could possibly stand against them three. And I see pity, for they at least do not want us to lose, but lose they think we will."

"You're a good one to bolster courage before a fight. I am grateful you're here, but I'll not keep with your way of thinking, for we have something much grander than they."

"Aye? And what's that?" Blagger looked curious.

"We've got right on our side, and we've got God."

"Aye, that is a better place to keep our thoughts. But I've only been bringing things round, in my way, to more of my father's advice. You see, he also used to say, 'Don't meet force with force if the stronger of the two forces isn't your own.' So, maybe we could avoid their weapons by refusing to fully engage. We could continually harass them from all sides; one of us retreats as they attack, yet another of our number advances from the side, only to retreat himself as the giant turns his attentions there, and finally, we strike our own blow when their frustration causes them to make some misstep—"

"Hush!" Fergus interrupted. "Something happens."

A trap door in the middle of the arena unexpectedly swung open.

There was a faint intake of breath from the multitude of the assembly; it echoed strangely from so many voices, sounding almost like a whispering wind. All eyes watched the dark opening with fevered anticipation; the final battle of the games was about to begin.

Seconds passed, when suddenly a thickset dwarf seemed to be tossed up from below, shield outstretched before him, he tucked and rolled over it and then up into a crouch; his battleaxe swinging first left and then right. Not a sound from the crowd, still they held their collective breath.

The dwarf spun slowly round looking for danger, yet for now there seemed to be none. What spectacle would they make of the poor dwarf? Fergus felt for the man, alone as he was, without others to stand by him. He almost called out to encourage him, when something about the dwarf's manner evoked a familiar vision to mind, that of Gimcrack hunted by the Lyftfloga, and his sinking in the bog.

At that moment the dwarf turned in his direction, and Fergus saw that he was facing that very man; it was Gimcrack who stood upon the arena floor, brandishing an axe and a panicked look that Fergus had most assuredly seen before.

Before Fergus had recovered from his surprise, a second trap door opened, and the nervous dwarf ran to hide behind it, raising his axe in readiness for whatever might come out after him.

The experience had left Fergus strongly affected, for it brought him back to glad days when he had fought alongside his master, in fact, he fancied that he could almost hear McDougal now. It was as if Lord McDougal was singing somewhere in Heaven, and God was allowing Fergus to hear that deeply missed voice. Was it a portent that he would soon be joining him?

Something was rising out from the floor. A large stone sarcophagus emerged, bleak and forbidding. The dwarf peeked out from behind the trap door.

A hand reached up from inside the stony tomb and grasped the edge. Another hand raised a sword to the sky. He had seen that sword before. There was a lump in Fergus's throat and he held his breath; he gripped the portcullis until his knuckles turned white.

Then a voice spoke clear and strong from within the sarcophagus, "It's a sky like this that puts you in awe of your Creator."

The man pulled himself to a sitting position; his wild red hair reflected the sun. His smile shone even brighter.

Fergus brought the back of his hand to his face and dabbed at the corners of his eyes where something wet was bothering his vision.

The four portcullises of the arena began to rise.

Homage Given

Lord McDougal climbed out of the sarcophagus and stretched his legs. The portcullises reached their height.

McDougal was laying his hand gently on the shoulder of Gimcrack, but whatever he said was drowned out as trumpet blasts filled the air.

The giants paused just outside their gate.

McDougal and Gimcrack walked over to where Fergus and Blagger stood. Igi Forkbeard, Oded and Ubaldo were coming their way.

The trumpeters lowered their instruments.

McDougal smiled his boyish grin. "I've a mind to greet you with a proper bear-hug, Fergus, but I won't. I don't suppose you'd like this many people watching your lord behave in such a way."

"Thank you, sir." Fergus was still stunned at seeing McDougal alive, and he didn't know quite what to say. "Are you aware, sir, what is about to happen?"

"I am. And it is good to have you at my side."

"It is, sir. I'm very much interested in hearing how you came to be here."

"When we've time, I'll gladly share the tale. Not at all pleasant, Fergus; it was a downright hurlothrumbo of a scary thing they did with me; a good opportunity to fly into the arms of God though, it was that." McDougal looked intently upon his face. "I've missed you, Fergus. You seem to be well."

"I am, sir."

"Shall we be about the business of saving Lady Mercy then?"

"Yes, sir … I'm sorry, sir. I did my best, but as you can see they've taken her from me."

"None of it, Fergus. With God's help, let's just teach them some proper manners. It's a dreadful way to treat women-folk. They ought to be ashamed."

"Very good, sir."

The others had arrived and stood waiting. McDougal looked upon each of the men before him, "Igi, Oded, Ubaldo, Gimcrack, Fergus, and …?"

"This is Blagger, sir," Fergus explained. "A good man, sent by Lord Tostig."

"And Blagger then. Welcome my friends. I will lean upon you as friends indeed, able warriors and counselors to speak as you will, but all battles require a captain. Will you acknowledge me as such? If not, choose another, and quick, I will follow or lead, whichever you like."

In unison the men bent their knees before Lord McDougal.

There was a slight vibration under their feet. The sarcophagus lowered as another pit opened, much larger and closer to the king's balcony. A chorus of beautiful voices sang from below, joined by stringed instruments, a rumbling of drums, and various flutes and pipes. The Master of Games climbed up from the pit.

He first stopped before the giants. Nothing could be heard of their discussion, but the Master of Games was dramatic in his movements, pointing towards the king, towards the music pit, towards the crowds, to archers on the walls, and finally to another pit opening near to where the Master of Games stood. A stone dais, twenty cubits round and two cubits high rose up from below. The giants stepped upon it, and held their weapons at rest.

The music kept on steadily as the Master of Games left the giants and approached the heroes. He bowed and eyed McDougal with something like awe and suspicion. "Lord McDougal 'dead no more', and good men of this company, in a moment another dais like the one you see the giants upon will emerge. This will be your starting place. All shall step upon it except for Lord McDougal 'dead no more', you sir, shall follow me to the king's balcony. He desires … to … um … ask of certain things before the battle, just in case you are unable to answer after its conclusion.

"Following the king's interview, you shall return to your dais, and await the arena's change. Do not leave the dais until the changes are complete or you may find yourself injured in the tumult. Five minutes will be allowed to study the lay of the new arena's floor and to plan for the melee—"

"Friendly counsel!" Oded interrupted, thrusting his open palm, quite large, before the face of the Master of Games and turned to Lord McDougal. Oded's lumbering voice was slow and steady, "I have something to say. Shall I say it?"

"Speak on, Oded," McDougal said grinning. Fergus realized that his master was never nonplused by great danger no matter what surprises came with it, and that he was enjoying himself grandly, regardless of the thousands watching, the wicked priests, the giants, the battle … he was childlike in his faith that God was there; so that he could watch and enjoy what God was up to with His people with relish and self-abandon. McDougal was safe in the arms of his Creator, whether that meant life or death. Fergus could not be sure that this was exactly what occurred in the mind and breast of his master, but it seemed very likely. What a marvel Lord McDougal was.

"Okay," Oded said. "I've dealt with these giants before and I don't know of any … well, Captain McDougal, I'd like to ask this fellow a question."

"Permission granted, Oded."

Oded dropped the hand which he held before the Master of Games, who was swallowing with difficulty. Oded was scratching his head. "That sounds a bit supicous to me. Are you ready for my question Master of Games?"

"I am." His head was bent almost perpendicular in order to look up into Oded's face.

"You said something about Maylay."

"Yes, I did."

"Who's Maylay?"

"Whose melee?" The Master of Games stared back confused, "Why, your melee, of course."

Oded pointed at himself incredulously. "I'm not Maylay … you're Master of Games. You ought to know I'm Oded, Oded the Bear."

The Master of Games suddenly comprehended the mistake. "No, not someone named Melee, I mean 'battle', your battle."

"I'm not Battle, didn't you just hear me tell you who I am?" Oded put his big hands in front of the startled man's face again and turned to McDougal. "Captain McDougal, this fellow's not right in the head. How will we know what's what if they send a fellow like this out to us?"

There was a twinkle in McDougal's eye as he responded, "Yes, Oded, well done. There are certainly things happening here that are not on the up and up, but we shall see them through, and cast a wary eye upon the proceedings. Yes?"

"Okay."

"I think you can let the man see us now, Oded."

"Okay." Oded removed his hand, but continued to stare as he shuffled his weight from side to side, furrowing his brows and leaning in towards the Master of Games.

"I will continue then," The Master of Games said as he tried to ignore the threatening motions of Oded. "The king shall fire an arrow at the opposite wall, and its consequent shattering shall mark the games commencement. Do you understand? Good—"

"No!" Oded's voice was like a thunderclap.

The Master of Games jumped.

Oded was scratching his head again. "Why is the king shooting at the games common's mint, and what are we supposed to do with the mint? Eat it I suppose?"

The Master of Games stared back uncomprehendingly.

"Very clever, Oded," McDougal said, "Don't let him side track you with talk of food. The important part is that when the king shoots his arrow, we get ready to fight."

"Oh." Oded scrunched his nose up. "I wouldn't eat any mints from this fellow anyway."

The Master of Games began to grow red in the face. "Yes, well then, here's your dais now. Remember, do not leave it until the king has commenced … I mean begun the games. If you'll follow me then, Lord McDougal 'dead no more'."

With that he bowed stiffly and walked to the king's balcony. As they approached, a stairway came up from the floor. Fergus followed quietly behind his lord, hoping no one would notice, at least until it would seem beyond tolerable decorum to send him back. He had made up his mind to stay as close to McDougal as possible, even if it meant stretching his role somewhat beyond the normal capacities of shield barer.

Rosencross had heard of Lord McDougal of course, but he had never seen him before, except on horseback and from a great distance. He was a strange man to look upon with his wild red hair, long neck and exceedingly long limbs. Could it be true that they had brought him back from the dead to do battle with the giants? Whether or not they had, it seemed very likely he would be dead again before the day was through; for he had not the appearance of a great warrior.

The witch Esla was hovering about the king; she was but one of many court magicians and necromancers sharing the balcony today. Rumors had been whispered and then spread only a few hours earlier that Esla and others had raised some great hero from the dead. The crowds were still so awed by its seeming veracity that they were uncommonly quiet as they watched every move that Lord McDougal made.

He was climbing steps to the balcony with one of his men following behind. The lady he had come to fight for, dressed in black, had not turned her head since Rosencross had arrived. Rosencross had only seen her from the side, but he had been somewhat charmed by her profile and her calm demeanor. Not entirely calm it seemed, for now she was placing her hands beneath a fold in her robes — before they had disappeared, he saw them trembling. But her smile was radiant as she looked upon McDougal.

The king trembled also, and he leaned forward in his seat. "You look very much like Lord McDougal. Is it truly you?"

"It is I, my King, though—"

"Hah," King Strongbow turned on the witch Esla and grasped her hand, "I knew you could do it …" his eyes gleamed, they seemed to abandon this world for a moment before returning, and then he addressed McDougal once again. "Tell me! Tell me! What was it like in the grave? And where did you travel when dead? Have you any special powers? Did the gods speak of me? My mother, was she there? Speak, at once, speak!"

Lord McDougal bowed low. "Sire, I am very much alive, because the God of Noah has willed it so. I did not die, as I can see that you've been led—"

"Lies!" The king leapt to his feet. He clenched his fists on either side of his face and stared at Lord McDougal. Seconds passed. He clenched and unclenched his fists. No one dared move. Then he slumped into his seat and waved his hand as at a gnat. "This is what they said you would say, McDougal 'dead no more', that you would not likely recall anything, so I suppose I cannot be angry with you.

"Oh, but how I wanted to see beyond the veil. Mayhap your memories will come back, and when they do, I command you as your king to tell me first of your travels — when you traveled beyond the veil as McDougal 'the dead'."

"My King, I am here today at your request to fight for the purity of the Lady Mercy. She, who has loved you and your family, your friends and even your lowest servant. She has served you as only one who loves God first and foremost can.

"I found her amongst the false priests of false gods: evil spirits, demons parading amongst mankind to lure them from the one true God. Before Him, I acknowledge myself as her champion and protector. In His hands I place myself, whether to win the day or not, it is for Him to decide, and me to accept, with faith and joy upon my heart.

"And to you, Lady Mercy, I thought to encourage and counsel, that you might run to the arms of the living God. Not to hope in me or the men who gather below for your defense, but to hope in the God of Noah, no matter what the day may bring. But, I can see by the light in your eye, my sweet lady, that God has touched you with this truth ere I arrived — yea, but it strengthens me and encourages me. Thank you, dear Mercy. And if God sees fit to strengthen our arms with victory, I would very much like that cup of tea."

Lord McDougal bowed deeply before Mercy, and only a little less deeply before the king. He turned slowly and descended the stairs.

The priests, magicians, necromancers and Esla protested, but not with open rebuke. No, they grumbled quietly, glared, and their skin turned a burning red.

The king kept waving his hand and then looked about confused. He blinked his eyes thrice, almost as if he were trying to wake himself from a dream.

Princess Catrina called out, loud enough for even McDougal to hear as he neared the bottom of the stairs. "Never have I seen such a foppish man. I have personally seen him trip over many a word and many a chair, his glass spilling upon his lap, his left foot tripping upon his right, and his exaggerated sense of self tripping worst of all when he dared think to court me, the king's daughter. I laughed then behind closed doors, and I laugh at him now, openly."

McDougal paused. Catrina gloated over him, until she saw him turning around. At once she swallowed, lengthening her neck as if it were difficult to do so. Her back straight and her head held high, she would not look in his direction. Her face was suddenly pale.

"You speak rightly of me," McDougal said, his voice heavy with sadness. "You were a flower much too lofty to set my eyes upon. Please forgive me my mistake."

She did not speak again until he was well out of earshot. "He makes me sick to look upon, unless it is to laugh at him when he stumbles or stutters." Now that McDougal was far enough away, many of the priests, magicians, and nobles were brave enough to snicker and mock in response.

The Lady Mercy at once stood up and looked around at all those who laughed. When her eyes fell upon Rosencross he clutched at his breast, for the resemblance to his late wife, the Countess Johanna, was astonishing. But the words she then spoke were what strengthened the likeness far greater, for they were words that Johanna would have spoken if she had still lived.

Exhortation

Mercy's small form bloomed before the king and all her priestly antagonists; her words held beauty and power, despite a slight quiver in her voice, because the words came from a place of decency, of goodness, and of truth.

"My King, my father's brother. I have lived in your home these past years, and you have, with grace, taken me in as a member of your family, and at times I can attest that you have loved me, at times you have bathed me in kindness; but I have watched as wicked ones have, in turn, bathed you with flatteries and froward counsel whispered in your ears.

"Think back my King; they were things your counselors would not have dared to say had they been spoken in the light, before honest men. My father, your brother, used to say, 'Let not an evil speaker be established in the earth; evil shall hunt the violent man to overthrow him.'

"But I look about you, my King, and evil speakers flourish; their roots grow like a weed about your person, and their poison spreads as a canker."

King Strongbow stopped waving his hand and looked upon her with unseeing eyes. Then he looked back to the retreating form of McDougal and he smiled, and then he looked around at the crowds and he continued to smile. He spoke then, not as one who has just been corrected, but as one who has received adoration, devotion, even deification.

His face was radiant, "Yes, my brother would have been proud. I have done something so grand, so memorable, that even if these heroes lose the day, my games will be talked of through the centuries … the one who brought men back from the dead. I have raised the dead."

Count Rosencross looked quickly over the faces of the magicians and necromancers to see what was written upon their faces. For they had been given the credit just moments before for raising Lord McDougal from the dead, and now the king had not even mentioned them; in fact he seemed to think that he had done it by himself. Their faces gave nothing away. Rosencross thought them wise statesmen indeed.

But, the witch Esla was not hiding her thoughts well, perhaps she was still stirred up by Lady Mercy, who had essentially called her an 'evil speaker.' Esla's face was very pale, she grimaced … but was there more to it than malice … she swayed some and caught hold of the king's seat.

No one spoke. The king was smiling to himself. A movement from Mercy caught the Count's attention. He was struck by her countenance as she looked upon the king;

it was clear that she loved him; the rebuke she had given was to call him home, to right, to love … *just as my Johanna used to call to me.*

Esla was falling. In an instant, Rosencross leapt from his seat and caught her. She had not blacked out, but her head lolled and fell against his cheek. Her skin was terribly warm. He set her down in his own seat, and she leaned back into its embrace without threatening to fall further; still her face was ashen and her eyes glossed. It had all happened so quickly, and Rosencross moved with such agile grace that hardly any took notice of the incident.

Mercy looked round at all who had mocked Lord McDougal; even now her appearance had the air of sincerity, of sympathy, and of hope. "You, whose derisive laughter still echoes in this place. I look at you and then at that noble warrior of God who walks across the arena to stand for truth and honor and for the weak. And I am amazed that you cannot see your own vileness; the pit that you lay for others, how it will, in the end, be the dark pit of which you shall fall into yourselves."

Tears slowly wetted her eyes. Rosencross was sure that she did not cry for herself or for the heroes destined to die before the giants; but that she was crying for the priests and nobles, and he was among them — he was one of them for whom she cried.

She continued, "Must I remind you, dear sirs, that the giants have allowed for twenty men to fight them, and yet I count only seven ... why are those numbers not increased? Why are not the nobles of our land swelling the ranks of those heroes below? Surely not fear, for I know there are no cowards among the king's noble knights. What then? Can it be a disregard for the cause of a lady? A condescension upon the High King of Heaven's laws of right and wrong? A contempt for the honor of our kingdom? Are those seven men the last of our heroes, whose breasts are filled with chivalry and truth?

"I am at a loss to know what keeps you from strengthening the arms of your fellows. I fear for the women and children of this land, when the men of rank take evil for good and good for evil. The weak shall cry to their God; and glory be to Him, He hears our cries. I will die today if those men lose. But what will die in you if you sit by and do nothing? I do not just call you to action for this day, but I call you to God Himself, to Elohiym, to the God of Noah."

Lady Mercy turned her back on those to whom she spoke, and sat.

The king's platform was very still.

What a beastly crossroads Count Rosencross felt himself upon. He knew the stirrings of it. This choice to follow after the things of Elohiym or after the gods and the god of self. Here it was again, before him like a chasm opening wider every second, the edges were spreading with one foot on each side. He must act, he must move to one side or the other. Something told him that this was his last chance. He thought that he had made this decision long ago, but here was that old pricking of his heart, pangs that felt as real as any two edged sword cutting him asunder from within. With a start, he remembered when those first stabs had reappeared in his life — at least with the kind of conscience rending power to awaken the deadness within him — it was when Suzie had sung of her God, but even more notably, was the night he stood upon the roof of their abandoned tower, when he heard Thiery reading or reciting from the book called Job.

Those words … it was almost as if they were alive and stronger than anything he had ever known … *stronger than the Dragon?*

Suddenly his heart was pounding.

Earlier, he had watched her with curiosity, not really caring what the day would bring, but now … he very much wanted her to live. He came to his feet, passed Lady Mercy, stepped over the barricade, and descended the steps into the arena.

He heard the gentle voice of Lady Mercy from behind him, "Most noble knight … may God bless and keep you."

He almost laughed at the ridiculous title, for suddenly he was seeing himself in a new light; and he saw that he, of all people, was far from noble. But the words of the virtuous lady — so much like his Johanna — were also soothing. He alone, of all the king's platform, had been spoken to in such a way, and by her.

The Change

The crowds cheered as the warrior in black leather descended into the arena. Before he had reached bottom, the stairs began to sink into the arena floor from which they had emerged. He leapt from them, only to have the planking in front of him disappear.

Planks fell away like an earthquake's fissure gaping towards the sky with unknown and fearsome depths below, forming a narrow pit, a few cubits wide, which ran fully around the entire arena. As it yawned open the warrior in black jumped over, and then hundreds of hands reached up from below and grabbed, yet longer flooring planks — about thirty feet long, extending all the way back to the perimeter wall — and quickly dragged them down into the dark.

There was a sound of rushing water. In a short time the arena became an island surrounded by a thirty foot canal, a river of clear, still water. Then another canal split the island down the middle making it two islands, one for the heroes and one for the giants.

The crowd grew more excited with each revelation; sometimes they would gasp, sometimes clap and sometimes cheer. Within a quarter of an hour, a thousand workers finished the arena's staging: a bridge connecting the two islands: a single-masted cog adrift upon the waters, her rounded bows and deep hull, with squared fore and aftercastles, was strange to behold so far from its natural element of the sea: massive boulders were strewn about: a large briar-patch on the heroes' island with dwarf size tunnels cut through it: and lastly, a maze of quagmires near the giants' dais.

The warrior in black was stranded on the giants' island until the workers finished the bridge. He stood waiting, a hand on his hilt and an eye on the giants.

Gimcrack shuddered. "Lord McDougal, that is Count Rosencross of Banockburn. The one who brought those creepy Dragon Priests among us."

Blagger spoke up, "And he's the one who poisoned Sir Tostig and we his men, when he pretended to drink a toast to our health. He's a devious one." Fergus was grateful that Tostig himself was not here — he had been sent on an errand of the Chroniclers — but as it was he could see and appreciate the turmoil fermenting within Blagger. It was also clear where the thoughts of Gimcrack were taking him. As the Count crossed the bridge, Gimrack stepped behind McDougal.

Igi Forkbeard added his assent, "Yes, and I've fought alongside him. He's a dangerous man to make your enemy. I've seen precious few draw their weapon so fast, or wield it with such skill."

"Well, my friends," McDougal said, "he's coming now. Blagger has the only proof of wrong doing, but we haven't the time, nor is this the place to address such things. I'll ask you to be silent while we hear what it is he wants."

Count Rosencross stopped before the heroes' dais, his head held proudly; but something in his face showed that he knew his welcome was less than he had expected. Finishing touches upon the arena left fewer and fewer workers in view. There was not much time now, and what time there was, Fergus knew, should be spent with McDougal encouraging them, and telling them just what his plans were.

"I'm asking myself, and asking God," McDougal began, addressing the Count, "What does this man's presence here mean? And how should I receive him? I shall be blunt, for circumstances require it. Count Rosencross, words have come to my ears of underhandedness concerning you and my friend, Lord Tostig, and yet I have also heard how you sought after the safety of young Suzie, of whom I am protector. I think on these things, Count, and I wonder.

"The crowds cheered as you entered the arena; and I know that the Lady Mercy has won their hearts; shall I assume as they do, that you've come to defend her in battle against the giants?"

"I have." The Count's proud look did not waiver.

"I perceive, and perhaps wrongly, that you, Count Rosencross, are a man caught between two opinions. For the moment at least you lean towards truth. Two children of

God, Suzie and Lady Mercy, have shined God's light upon you, and you have been moved to intercede on their behalf.

"I receive you then as one of us in this fight, but I beg you to look beyond them whom you champion, and seek the living God who caused Mercy and Suzie to shine in such a way as to attract your nobler attentions. Do you accept me as your captain in this fight, as these men have? Or do you choose to make your own way?"

Rosencross hesitated. He looked at each of the men.

There were only a dozen workers left on the arena floor and they were making their way to various trap doors. There was little time left.

Igi stepped forward. "Lord McDougal, if you like, I could act as shield barer for the Count. We each know the others' ways; we fight well together."

"Let it be so then," McDougal said. "Count? Does this suit you?"

Some dark storm played upon the features of Rosencross. For an instant it almost seemed as if someone stood next to him, whispering in his ear; twice he began to turn towards the unseen person, and twice he pushed at the space next to him with his white gloved hand. It was strange behavior.

"God bless us with wisdom, Count," McDougal said, almost imploring. "God bless us with sound minds. He establishes the thoughts of him whose ways are set on God."

A worker descended below the arena. His hand reached back into the light, set an hourglass upon the ground and flipped it over; then the last of the trap doors closed. The sand began to fall. Five minutes left, and the crowd was once again still.

Rosencross eased some, nodded his head ever so slightly to McDougal, and without a word stepped upon the dais. Fergus caught the look in Blagger's eye and watched him shift uncomfortably.

McDougal laid his plans before them. "By no means engage face to face. Only Oded and Ubaldo would have a chance of meeting the strength behind their weapons. They shall be their own detachment, Fergus and I a detachment, and the Count and Igi another. Blagger and Gimcrack will be by themselves; their task is to be always moving, hiding, appearing, approaching, running; only attacking if they've a clear way to make a strike, and then only to retreat again — we must keep them guessing.

"Have you ever seen dogs bating a bear, how they worry at him and tire him, so that the hunter may strike with less danger to himself? We must all be as the dogs for each other. But it will be Gimcrack and Blagger's especial role. The giants must be bated — every turn to look for you, or swipe in your direction, will give the rest of us a chance.

"Do not look so glum, Blagger, our success depends upon your ability to carry out this charge."

"Yes, sir," Blagger said contritely. "It's a good plan, sir, and I'll not let you down."

Gimcrack raised his axe. "And neither will I, sir."

McDougal laid a hand upon Gimcrack's shoulder. "I know you won't, my friend, and I'll be needing an inventor for what I've in store. The first thing I'll have you do is gain access to the ship. I can see two ropes over her sides. She's very near the canal that divides our two islands. See if you can't first pull her into it, and then climb aboard."

Fergus saw Gimcrack become exceedingly attentive and motionless; his mouth hung open, his eyes were wide and bright — with an occasional twitch.

"And this is most important," McDougal continued, "you must cut away the sail and lower the boom so that it just clears the fore and aftercastles. I want her to swivel freely in any direction; cut the necessary riggings. But make sure she'll not come free of the mast. Now, you see how they've catheaded the anchor to her hull; if you've the time, remove it and tie it off to the end of the boom. When you've finished that, disappear over her side and continue to harass our foe.

"Do you understand everything I've said?"

Gimcrack's eye twitched.

McDougal winked back. "Good. Now, we've only a few minutes. A prayer to our Creator is what we're needing now—"

"Oh, oh," Oded interrupted. "My brother is a right good prayerer. Can he pray for us? I can interpret what he says."

King Strongbow had not shot the arrow that would begin the melee, yet Ogre had stepped down from his dais and was inspecting the bog-pits; testing the ground with his weapon — a gigantic tree limb studded with iron spikes.

Now that the time was growing short, Ogre stationed himself in front of the bridge and raised his weapon menacingly, ready to charge across at the breaking of the arrow. Goblin bellowed from the dais, coaxing Ogre to feats of slaughter.

Lunace, bare to the waist, flexed his massive torso as he turned his two-handed sword this way and that, growling with each pose — the veins on his face and neck protruded, and his face turned an ugly red until he let out his breath only to repeat the fearful spectacle.

"Of course. Ubaldo's prayer will be a balm for our souls." McDougal bowed his head. The others followed suit.

Fergus decided to pray with his eyes open. The giants were working themselves into a frenzy and he feared they might not wait for the king's signal. The archers on the walls seemed to be of the same mind, for many pulled back arrows in readiness.

Ubaldo raised his hands to heaven and closed his eyes. His face, usually so wooden and stoic, softened, then stirred with enthusiasm, as if the muscles of his face attempted to imitate the movements of his hands.

Goblin stopped yelling and clutched an idol hanging about his neck. Ogre stopped waving his tree limb. Lunace let out his breath in mid pose.

Oded interpreted, "Dear Heavenly Father, every man is brutish in his knowledge: every founder is confounded by the graven image: for his molten image is falsehood, and there is no breath in them. They are vanity, and the work of errors: in the time of their visitation they shall perish; the gods that have not made the heavens and the earth, even they shall perish from the earth, and from under these heavens."

Goblin was yelling again. "Incantations! Spells! They're putting a spell upon us!"

"But the LORD is the true God, He is the living God, and an everlasting King: at His wrath the earth shall tremble, and the nations shall not be able to abide His indignation ."

Ogre was whirling his studded tree above his head.

Ubaldo continued his prayer, "He hath made the earth by His power, He hath established the world by His wisdom, and hath stretched out the heavens by His discretion. When He uttereth His voice, there is a multitude of waters in the heavens; He maketh lightnings with rain, and bringeth forth the wind out of His treasures—"

"Everyone down!" Fergus shouted the command just as Ogre let go and his tree-club hurtled through the air.

They were men accustomed to battle; life or death was often decided by an instant; swift was their reaction. They hit the ground, and rolled off the dais. All but one of them.

Ubaldo stood with his closed eyes to heaven, a visage of joy and peace upon his face. He could hear no command.

A Bad Beginning

Ogre's tree-club was about ten feet long and thick as a man's waist at its widest. It flew through the air, end after end, spinning wildly.

Ubaldo never knew what hit him; the weapon glanced off his head, an iron spike tore a gash above his ear, and still the tree-club continued on its terrible path, finally careening over the water and striking the arena's wall with a thud.

Ubaldo crumpled to the ground, unmoving.

King Strongbow leapt to his feet, barking commands to his archers.

A murmur buzzed through the stadium like a swarm of angry bees.

The heroes crowded around their fallen companion. Oded's head swung back and forth. "No … no … no … Ubaldo? Can you hear me?"

He lay there deathly still.

"No … no … no …"

Igi and Fergus straightened Ubaldo's limbs and head, and rolled him onto his back.

"No … no … Ubaldo? Ubaldo? It's me, Oded."

McDougal tore a piece of his shirt as a bandage to stop the bleeding above Ubaldo's ear.

"No … no … no …"

Gimcrack turned to glance nervously at the giants. This was a bad beginning. He heard Goblin laughing from their dais.

"You got 'em, Ogre," Goblin chortled, rubbing his idol and amulets. "The gods are with us." He moved to step from the dais; Strongbow's arm came down, and a torrent of arrows spattered the ground before Goblin's feet. Goblin froze.

After throwing his tree-club, Ogre had followed behind, crossing the bridge onto the heroes' island. He clenched his now empty hands; empty of any weapon; his victorious smile turned to a scowl as he looked up at the score of archers with bows trained his way. He took a cautious step back towards the bridge.

The king's arm came down. Bows twanged. Arrows cut through the air and sunk into the planking at Ogre's feet.

"No … no …" Oded groaned. But he was no longer looking at his brother's broken and bleeding body. Oded's eyes narrowed and fixed on Ogre. He whispered, just loud enough for Gimcrack to hear, something about unfair play and a net of wickedness.

Ogre returned Oded's stare and smiled mockingly. They were separated by fifty paces, no obstacle barred their path. Gimcrack's stomach knotted with a queer coldness.

Something must have broke deep inside Oded; Gimcrack sensed a change come over him, he saw Oded's muscles tense, and then, like a bear robbed of its cubs, hair bristling, a deep rumble in his chest, he thundered from the dais. His great war-hammer lay where he left it, its handle pointing to the sky.

Before any of the heroes could react, a shower of arrows swiftly sought the ground, making an ominous barricade between them and the fight Oded was rushing towards.

The buzzing of the crowds quieted. King Strongbow, upon his platform, leaned over its parapet.

Ogre eased forward, one leg back, and with his two powerful arms extended to receive Oded's charge, he grinned. Oded seemed to get bigger right before impact, his body bristling, he raised up higher and higher; Ogre's arms raised in degrees to meet his opponent. But when Ogre clamped his trap shut, to squeeze and crush, he found nothing but empty air.

At the last moment, with terrific speed, Oded dropped below Ogre's grasp and buried his shoulder into the forward leg of the brutish giant. Even Ogre's tree like limbs could not sustain such a blow without breaking upon the impact. But Ogre had not been entirely taken in by the ruse; he shifted his weight back and up so that his leg gave way.

Oded smashed. The impact sent him flying to his left; he ducked his head and rolled over and up to his feet. Ogre's body seemed much too heavy to leave the ground, but his leg flew back carrying the rest of his body with it like a windmill. He flipped over and landed hard. But he too was up and on his feet in a second. They circled warily.

Ogre limped as he moved. Yet, even with his damaged leg, it seemed an uneven contest. For Ogre was over twelve feet tall, and Oded only nine. They were equally barrel-chested and thick of limb, but Ogre outweighed him by a hundred and fifty pounds, and his reach was at least a foot greater.

With no other weapons than their arms, legs, and hands they fell to with fisticuffs. Gimcrack knew — seeing Oded both in battle and in contests arranged by Count Rosencross — that Oded had made up for his slowness of mind with diligent training in matters of war, even those basic methods of combat such as body-throwing and pugilism.

Those contests, though, were usually for the training of men, or amusements of the camp; and Oded's gentile heart shrank from truly harming a soul. Yet, he was a force to be reckoned with, and with such ability, that Gimcrack had learned to fear the possibilities behind others — perhaps they might also hide their speed and skill as Oded did.

Ogre stepped in swinging, left then right. Oded dodged the first and retreated as the second glanced off his chin. Immediately he stepped forward under another swing and struck hard at Ogre's ribs.

Ogre moved in as if to swing again, then pivoted his hip, and struck out with a vicious kick at Oded's leg. He grimaced as he did so, his own bad leg giving him trouble. Oded stepped into the kick and raised his knee into Ogre's other thigh. Ogre howled and staggered. Oded followed with two more strikes to the body. They bore down on each other then, raining blows like shots discharged by the twisted cords of a catapult.

It seemed impossible for any man to receive even one of those fists, yet they both took and gave many. Ogre was beginning to sway. Oded ducked under another swing, blasting a pummel to the body: with a collective summons of his swelling muscles and his hardened frame following behind his arm, Oded poured the pile-driving might of his fist into Ogre's ribs.

There was an audible crack.

But Ogre absorbed the blow and pulled his arms tight around Oded, lifting him from the ground in a bear-hug. One arm bent before him, and the other straight at his side, Oded could not get leverage with his feet, nor break free with his arms. The two pillars of epic strength stared into each others' eyes, and Ogre began to squeeze.

The giant's neck bulged as he held his breath to crush all the harder. Oded's face began to redden and then his head hung slightly.

The heroes made to move from their platform. More arrows flew to block the way.

Oded's head fell farther and farther forward until it leaned against Ogre's chest. But Ogre had to take a breath and when he did, he relaxed some, so that Oded's fist came up. Yet only half way before Ogre's breath was taken, and the punishing vise of his arms constricted once again; Oded's fist caught between them.

Again Oded's head lolled to the side, the redness of his face deepening its hue. It was a terrible thing to watch without lifting a hand to help their friend. Gimcrack was praying, no, begging God, to intervene. Everything was still and quiet, except for the grunts from Ogre's mouth. He too looked done in.

Suddenly there was another crack.

Maybe Oded wasn't so slow of mind after all. Had he lifted his fist purposefully between them, so that when Ogre resumed his deathly squeeze he had snapped his own ribs. He would have at least two broken ribs now.

Ogre howled and dropped his arms, looking stunned.

Oded fell to his knees, his chest heaving. Ogre started to raise his fist for a blow, but instead he howled again and let his arm fall limply to his side. He turned back to the bridge and cried out with every step, soon he was whimpering, even his breathing looked painful. Once on the giants' island, moving slow and deliberate, he eased himself to the ground and rolled onto his back; his face was contorted in agony.

The color came back into Oded's face. He stood. The crowds cheered. As he walked back to the heroes' dais, they continued to cheer.

King Strongbow raised his bow and let loose an arrow.

Melee

Strongbow's arrow shattered upon the arena's far wall. The melee had officially begun.

Ogre was out; now they had only two giants left of which to contend. But at what price? Ubaldo was also out. The bleeding had stopped and he breathed still, but he showed no signs of awakening from his giant induced slumber. Oded looked battered; he glanced down at his brother, a sadness in his eyes. He picked up his shield and war hammer, ready to follow McDougal's commands.

Blagger ran from the dais. Throwing himself upon his belly, he disappeared into the briar patch. Gimcrack remembered his task now; stomach flipping, heart pounding, his mouth dry, he looked at the ship — two of his worst fears: water and boats. Why hadn't he said something to McDougal when he had the chance? But it was too late now.

McDougal and the other heroes spread out. They were counting on Gimcrack to get that ship and prepare it for … well he didn't really know what for, but it was the task given to him, and he knew he'd better set about performing it. Their lives and the life of Lady Mercy might depend upon it.

The giants were moving cautiously towards the bridge. If he didn't hurry, they might cut him off; moreover, the ship was getting dangerously close to the center canal; he must use its momentum to guide it into place, but if it were to pass the crossroads, no strength of his was going to pull it back.

The time was now. Gimcrack's feet wouldn't move. *Oh God, not again, I'm such a coward and all the world can see it. Please help me … oh, what were those words … yes, now I remember:*

'Why art thou cast down, O my soul? And why art thou disquieted within me? Hope thou in God: for I shall yet praise Him. The LORD is my light and my salvation; whom shall I fear? The LORD is the strength of my life; of whom shall I be afraid?

'When the wicked, even mine enemies and my foes, came upon me to eat up my flesh, they stumbled and fell.

'Though an host should encamp against me, my heart shall not fear.

'When Thou saidst, Seek ye my face; my heart said unto thee, Thy face, LORD, will I seek.'

Gimcrack ran straight for the ship, only he left too late. Lunace stepped onto the bridge rail and launched himself at an angle over the last remaining feet of the canal. He landed before the path of the frantic dwarf.

Lord McDougal had said for him not to engage the enemy; the command was no more needed than if he had been told to stay away from the beastly Dragon Priests. Some things were obvious beyond the need of mentioning.

Gimcrack veered towards the briar patch. Lunace's sword swung to intercept him. Gimcrack lunged backwards, rolling. When he came to his feet, Goblin was already behind him, swinging a curved war hammer.

Again, Gimcrack dropped into a roll, screaming, "Whom shall I fear?!"

The sword and hammer came down with alarming rapidity; this only spurred Gimcrack on to convulsive feats of dexterity, inspired by his hope in the God of Noah, by fear, and by the knowledge of just how hard it was to strike a man who refused to fight back — whose sole purpose it was to escape each blow.

"Whom shall I fear?!" Gimcrack danced.

"Hope thou in God!" He rolled.

"Aagghh!" He jumped.

"You came to eat me!" He ducked.

"But you'll stumble and fall! Aaagghh!" He twisted.

Goblin suddenly roared in pain; Fergus Leatherhead's hickory spear sticking from his shoulder.

Gimcrack was forgotten. All at once, the heroes struck at Lunace and Goblin from three sides. It was well that they had heeded McDougal's instructions to instantly retreat, for the answering attack of the giants was like an avalanche unleashed.

Lunace rushed upon Igi and the Count, but Igi was not as quick to draw back. Lunace swung.

Igi Forkbeard's sword and shield came up, but his sword broke and though his shield held true, it was thrust back into his own head with such force that he was felled with only one blow. Lunace was off and pursuing Count Rosencross. They were lost to Gimcrack's view, though he saw Blagger running hard behind.

Gimcrack made it to the ship. A heavy rope hung from the forecastle into the water; he caught it up with the beard of his axe, and pulled it to him, careful not to get too close to the edge. And then he began to pull the rope towards the center canal; slowly the ship turned her bow. Gimcrack watched and listened as he strained at the rope, his sides heaving.

Goblin gritted his teeth and tore the spear from his shoulder, he cried out, a red stain spread across his jerkin. He roared his battle cry, and drew back his good arm like a windlass levering the twisted skeins of a ballista's sinew; the hickory spear fully retracted, aimed at the back of its intended mark.

Fergus Leatherhead ran, McDougal at his side, ran also. There was a bellowing roar of triumph and agony, and Goblin's missile flew.

A flash of movement from behind the briars caught Gimcrack's eye, and then Blagger leapt into the spear's path, shield upraised before him. The blow struck, pierced the shield, and sent Blagger reeling to the ground. Goblin followed behind his throw switching his curved war hammer to his good hand. Grimacing, he jumped over Blagger's prostrate body and bore down upon McDougal and Fergus.

They split apart. Goblin didn't hesitate; he followed the man who had so painfully wounded him; Fergus was herded toward the canal and he had no choice but to turn and fight or jump into the water. But Fergus had only one other weapon, a short sword, hardly sufficient against the long reach of Goblin.

McDougal was doubling back round the heroes' dais to aid his friend.

Goblin howled his frustration, seeing Fergus pick up speed to leap far into the canal.

Goblin lifted his war hammer back behind his head and threw it with tremendous force. Fergus jumped.

It hit him hard from behind. Spinning in the air, Fergus struck the water on his face and disappeared beneath its surface. Goblin drew his broad sword — though in his hands it looked like a long dagger — and turned with a shout of exultation to hunt down his next foe.

He had not far to look, for McDougal was upon him, with such a flurry of attacks, feints, and counterattacks that Gimcrack could not tell one strike from another.

Goblin was bleeding in several places. Forced to retreat, he was now in danger of falling into the water himself.

Gimcrack forced his eyes from the battle, for the ship was fully turned into the center canal.

Tense, his upper teeth protruding as he drew his lips back and curled them up under his nose, he reached high on the rope — teeth twitching like a rabbit's — and he lifted his feet from the security of solid ground. Gimcrack's head wobbled back as he swung out over the water, he felt dizzy, the strength left his arms, and suddenly his toe dragged along the water's surface.

Water! The deep! The image of Fergus sinking beneath the dark blue came to his mind and then Gimcrack screamed, "Drowning! Oh God! Deliver me!" Still his head wobbled upon a neck that no longer worked as it should. How he wanted to put his feet upon the ground again; everything moved and swayed and made watery-wood creaking sounds and splashes.

My heart shall not fear … my heart shall not fear … my heart shall not fear …

Hand over hand he climbed the rope to the forecastle.

My heart shall not fear …

Before it seemed possible, his hand reached the top. He felt sure that the water sensed his pending escape. Was it reaching up after him?

Then he was over and safe.

His hands trembled violently. It was good that Gimcrack did not have to climb the mast in order to lower the boom — for Gimcrack did not particularly like heights. He worked quickly to cut away the sail and riggings and set the boom in place so that it could move freely. Gimcrack could see now what Lord McDougal might have had in mind. Upon the ship, the heroes would have a height advantage over the giants, though their weapons might not reach their target. But by reconfiguring the thirty foot boom to rotate upon the mast — with five feet of it extending beyond the mast — as a sort of hilt for a huge wooden sword, well, giant-like damage could be done to a giant's thick head.

He had forgotten to unlash the anchor and tie it to the boom. Leaning over the ship's bulwarks to cut the anchor free, he saw water lapping at the ship's hull; his head swooned. Fearful that he would topple over the side, Gimcrack gripped the rail, and stood back. Lord McDougal had said only to arrange the anchor if there was time for it, perhaps there was not time. He looked about the arena.

On the giants' island, Lunace dropped a dead or unconscious Count Rosencross into a bog-pit, feet first. Oded was in another bog, twisting and turning to free himself. Beyond him was Igi Forkbeard in yet another, already sunk up to his chest; his face was battered, but through his smashed lips he spoke, "Cease, Oded, you'll only make it worse."

Oded yielded to the mire; looking up at Lady Mercy on the king's platform, he began to cry.

On the heroes' island, Goblin's broad sword fell from his fingers, he dropped to his knees, his eyes rolled back, and then he fell forward at the feet of Lord McDougal.

McDougal was the only one left. He had single handedly defeated Goblin. He could do it again with Lunace and all would be well. Gimcrack prayed that it would be so.

Lunace turned and waited for Lord McDougal near the bogs. "It's very good of you to come to me, now I won't have far to cart you. I weary of carrying your men to my prison of sorts. If you don't die first, then you can join them, and watch as I'm awarded a hundred gold for each of them that I let live."

There was something about Lunace's eyes. It was as if they were windows into his soul — dark portals of lust and greed that threatened to grasp and pull you in.

He smiled cruelly. "Maybe the gold's not worth it. I don't know how you've bested Goblin, but I'm going to enjoy this." He talked big, but there was something in his manner that Gimcrack recognized easy enough. He was afraid.

McDougal had defeated Goblin, man to man — Lord McDougal 'dead no more'. That was it. Lunace was afraid because he believed he fought against something more than a man, something that had come back from the dead.

"Listen to me, giant Lunace, priest of Baal," McDougal commanded, lifting his sword toward the ship which had now moved by slow degrees until it had come to rest against the bridge. "Oh that men would praise the LORD for His goodness, and for His wonderful works to the children of men! Will you praise Him, giant Lunace?"

"I? A Cahna-Baal? A priest of the mighty Baal?! Your god is nothing next to him."

McDougal straightened, walked boldly across the bridge, and placed his back to the ship. "They that go down to the sea in ships, that do business in great waters; These see the works of the LORD, and His wonders in the deep. For He commandeth, and raiseth the stormy wind, which lifteth up the waves thereof. They mount up to heaven, they go down again to the depths."

Gimcrack was feeling a little sick.

McDougal continued, "He who made and moves the sea might move a mighty staff above my very head." McDougal's eye met for a second that of Gimcrack's. He winked. "And the wrath of that blow might knock you from your proud feet and into the prison-bog behind you, the very trap that you yourself have set. Do you not fear God in the least, like the sailor on the sea, in the tempest?"

"No."

Gimcrack, hands shaking, reached up to the hilt of the boom.

He understood Lord McDougal's meaning well enough. But Gimcrack's fingers were a hand-span short. The heavy 'blade' end of the boom had lifted the 'hilt' end higher than he expected. He could not reach it.

"The sailors," McDougal's face beamed, "they reel to and fro, and stagger like a drunken man, and are at their wits' end. Then they cry unto the LORD in their trouble, and He bringeth them out of their distresses.

"This may be your last chance, Lunace. Do you cry unto the Lord in your distress? Do you sense the heavy hand of God lifting his staff to strike you down? Will you repent?

"You fight in order that a woman shall die. It is murder. And it is evil. And it is sin. Again I ask, will you repent and turn to God, and yield this fight on her behalf?"

Gimcrack's heart was pounding, he searched in vain for something to stand upon, something to give him the leverage he needed to swing that great weapon. If only Lord McDougal would stop talking about sailors, and the sea, and waves.

Lunace's eyes shifted, beads of sweat trickled from his brow, yet it was a cool day. "I think that you are a fool, and that your god will not smite me with his staff. I will kill you, but first I will wait and see what your god can do. I think my god will stop the hand of yours."

Lunace spread his hands wide and waited. The crowds, unable to hear, began to murmur.

Gimcrack was beginning to panic when his eyes rested on an apparatus before him. Extending down between the ships rails were two large ropes, corded with a stout stick protruding from each. From them, a band extended back to a large stone, which in turn was set in a wooden trough, and pulled back the length of it. There were gears atop, and a swivel mount below, and a trigger …

Uncomprehending the import of what lay before him — for all he could think of was how he might move the boom to strike down the giant Lunace — he prayed that God would open his eyes. And then suddenly he knew.

Lunace began to laugh. He beat his chest with his free hand. His huge two handed sword lifted in the other.

Gimcrack held his breath; he'd never used one, but he'd seen others with them: it was a ballista, a large stone-throwing crossbow mounted to the ship's deck. Gimcrack knelt and peered down its length. He lifted the trigger end with trembling hands and slowly lined it up with Lunace's chest.

Lunace saw the movement and stopped laughing. His eyes squinted suspiciously.

Gimcrack fired.

The stone burst between the bulwarks and pulverized Lunace's free arm, shattering the bones. It fell limp and mangled at his side. He staggered back to the brink of the bog staring dumbly at his wound.

A cry of anger and agony burst from Lunace's lips, sending shivers through every hair upon Gimcrack's body, so that his limbs quivered and he clutched at his heart.

McDougal sprang forward in an instant. Lunace lifted his sword to strike, but he was too slow. McDougal crashed into the giant's chest. They tottered for a moment as Lunace tried to keep his ground. He dropped his sword and reached forward with his good arm as Lord McDougal jumped back.

The giant's long reach was just enough to seize hold of McDougal; together they fell into the bog-pit.

Gimcrack stared in horror.

The arena burst into a deafening roar of triumph.

The heroes had won. Gimcrack was the last man standing. They had won? He looked at the crowds. It was almost as scary as everything else he encountered.

As quick as they had erupted, the crowds roaring suddenly stopped, as if there was no air left for which they might take another breath.

What did it mean? Why were they so quiet?

Once again, Gimcrack's neck wasn't supporting his head very well. He must get off the ship. That must be the problem. Ships were bad.

"Your turn, dwarf."

Gimcrack didn't like the sound of that, not at all, not one bit.

He turned around.

Ogre was standing, hunched over in pain with one hand to his ribs, but standing nonetheless, and he held Lunace's two handed sword.

Alone

Percival, five years old though small enough to be three, held the weight of the world upon his scrawny shoulders. Twice in the past year, he had heard Pip talking to others about his little brother's poorly condition. It took some figuring, but he found out that 'poorly condition' meant a person might die, and he could tell by Pip's reaction whenever a coughing fit wracked Percival's tiny frame, that Pip was mighty fearful for Percival's life.

Percival went to sleep every night hoping he'd wake, and woke every morning hoping he'd make it through the day, all so that Pip would not have to be sad. This was his most important job, one he found increasingly difficult.

But lately, he had found another job to give some attention to, a job which he liked very much.

In Percival's world there were those who had stuff and wanted more, and there were those who had stuff and gave some of it away — a little anyway. Nobody had less than he and Pip. But for the first time in his young life, he had contributed to others, and he loved the feeling that it gave him.

The big man in black leather, whom he was sure God had sent, had given him a bag full of stuff: shoes, a jacket, all sorts of food … and when he had laid the food before Suzie and said she could have it to help with the meals, her eyes got big. She kissed him on the forehead and hugged him. But best of all, she said "God blessed us this day through you, Percival, and oh how He loves a cheerful giver."

Well, Percival felt cheerful all over, even his toes felt cheerful at the giving; so he decided that for the rest of his life he'd look for ways to be a giver.

Percival rolled over and yawned. Morning was mostly gone. Sunlight warmed the chamber. He peered over his bed and smiled; Horatio was dozing next to him and Suzie was busy around the pantry, humming. That cheerful feeling swelled up inside his chest. It felt a lot better than those coughing fits or those lonely days staring big eyed into the hearts of people as they passed his begging cup.

Until now, Pip had been the only one to swell Percival's heart to cheeriness. Yet he was often gone, trying to make a way for them, trying to get food for them. Now there was Master Gimcrack who had been very kind and he had invited them as guests to this wonderful tower; they had never been house-guests anywhere before.

And there was Thiery — tall, strong and sure, but kind and gentle too; Percival wasn't used to those qualities so evident in the same person, especially a young person. Thiery was always patient with him and eager to tell Percival about the God of Noah ... it was wonderful to behold how his eyes sparkled when he talked of his God. Yes, Thiery — along with Pip — was fast becoming a kind of hero to the little boy.

Then there was the big man from God, all dressed in black leather armor with a fancy sword — Percival desperately wanted to see him again and thank him and be brave before him. And Horatio, who followed him around everywhere was like a dream come true; Pip and Percival had never even left the walls of Hradcanny, so having a giant wolf befriend him, one he could play with and ride, was so exciting that he sometimes felt his heart might burst.

But by far his most favorite friend, of his now many favorite friends, who had suddenly and unexpectedly entered Percival's life, was Suzie. Her every look held a smile or a kind word, and she hugged him and kissed his forehead often. At night, she put him to bed with a song. She ran to him whenever he coughed or had trouble breathing, concern and love widening her eyes and tilting her head and running her gentle fingers through his hair or even rubbing his back.

Percival would do anything for Suzie.

"Good morning, Suzie."

Suzie jumped. "Good morning, brave Percival." She glided to his bedside, felt his forehead with the back of her hand, and squeezed him tight. "Hungry?"

"Yes, please!" Percival glanced at the table, and saw a setting placed for him, only one. It did a boy good to see someone caring for him like that. He looked over at Gimcrack's bed. "Has he come back yet?"

"No. But I hope he will very soon."

"What will happen to us if he doesn't?"

"I don't know," Suzie said in a strange tone that suggested unease or sadness. Percival couldn't be sure which.

Percival had a sudden thought, a peaceful thought. "But God does. He knows. Right?"

"Oh, yes!" Suzie said, clasping her hands together. "He always knows. How wonderful to hear you say so, Percival. We ought always to remember that, and remind each other of it."

"I did good, huh?"

"Yes, very."

"But God does gooder, right? Gooder than everyone?"

"Yes."

"I love God." Percival climbed into his chair. "Where are Pip and Thiery?"

"They left early. They didn't want to wake you. But they said to say good bye and that you're to be my protector."

"You bet. Me and Horatio, we'll keep you safe … only …" Pip looked about at the Dwarven Brotherhood's weapons hanging on the wall.

"What is it?" Suzie asked.

"Well, I don't feel much like a protector without nothin' to protect you with." He looked hopefully at a heavy broadsword gleaming in the sunlight.

"We better not touch those without asking Gimcrack," Suzie said, gently.

Percival sighed.

"But I've heard Thiery say that a staff is as good as a sword or better," Suzie said, encouragingly. "After you break-fast you could find something in the rubble below."

He shoveled one bite after another into his mouth.

Suzie talked as he ate. "Your brother took Thiery back to the Oracle this morning, hoping he could get a position at the Citadel, and Pip was going to look for Diego Dandy-something-or-other. He was really hopeful about getting a job from him. Won't it be wonderful to see what God does?"

Percival nodded his head vigorously. But he couldn't spare any words while he ate; some kind of special staff was hidden somewhere in that mess below, and he had to hurry and get it before protecting was called for.

Suzie suddenly gasped, "Oh dear, I forgot to tell them about our candles. They said they might be back after the sun sets and you and I will be in the dark then; we've used the last candle. I sure don't like the dark."

Percival's head came up. He swallowed quick. "You won't be in the dark then, Suzie."

"How come?"

"They said I was to be your protector, I'm pretty much a knight now I suppose, and I'm not gonna sit by and see you just a sittin' in the dark hours before bed. That wouldn't be fittin'. Not with me at your side doing nothin' about it. I'd be ashamed."

"Well, what can you do?"

"Pip let me keep some coppers that man from God gave us. I'm gonna make you a present of some candles, only …" his face clouded for a moment, and then he lighted up like fire stoked by a strong breeze. "Yes, that will do. I don't like to leave you not protected. But this is what I'll do. I'll leave Horatio and I'll be askin' God for Him to keep an extra special eye on you. Then I'll go out and get the candles. Will that do, Suzie?"

"You boys are so brave and gentlemananly." Suzie clapped her hands and jumped from her seat.

"Yep." Percival nodded his head, a serious look on his little face.

"But, will you be safe out there alone?" Suzie asked, worried.

"As long as I look like I don't have nothin' then people mostly leave me alone. I won't wear my new shoes or my jacket."

"Oh, that's so smart. I never would have thought of that."

"Yep."

Percival bowed his head and closed his eyes. After a minute he opened them and walked to the top of the stairs, his back straight and important looking.

He looked over his shoulder as he descended. Suzie was holding Horatio and smiling; with a twinkle in her eye, she lifted her hand and waved.

Flemup and Elvodug rubbed their hands to keep them warm, and looked sullenly at each other. They had hated cooking for the Count's army, but the warmth of the kitchen seemed much better than this.

To make matters worse they were both hungry. They'd quarreled earlier, and Elvodug had stormed off to get their break-fast from the market. He came back only to find that Flemup had fallen asleep. He was sleeping when he should have been watching. Now they couldn't know who was in or out of the blasted tower, and they'd not know when it was safe to sneak in and kidnap Suzie.

Elvodug was furious, and Flemup, while avoiding his glaring stares, shot quick defiant glances of his own. Neither had touched the food. They had been locked in this misera-ble battle for the last three hours, when hunger finally bested Elvodug's anger.

"I suppose we'd better eat, you blarmy fool."

"Suppose so." Flemup shrugged his shoulders. "First we missed all of the games and now we've got a cold break-fast. What filth did ya get us?"

"Beef pot pie."

"Beef!?" Flemup hunkered down for another fight. "How'd we afford beef; purse is gettin' mighty light."

"It won't be light for long," Elvodug said with a greedy gleam in his eye. "I can practically taste the silver that'll be due us. I'm sick a waitin' around, we're gonna make our move soon, real soon."

Flemup took a big bite; pie drippings made his lips and beard glisten. He spoke with his mouth full, "I like the sound of that, I dearly do. But what about the priest, and what he said about nobody seein' anything, or else."

"You afraid of him?" Elvodug challenged.

"'Course not! You?"

"Nope, not even a tinge. Not even when it's dark and spooky."

"Yeah, me neither."

Now that Elvodug's belly was filled, he had other news just aching to be told. The problem was he liked knowing stuff Flemup didn't, but he wanted Flemup to know about his knowing more than him, which meant he had to tell him about it. And then he was back on the same footing as that dumb-wit. But he couldn't hold it in any longer.

"Got me some news when I went for the victuals."

Flemup lifted one eyebrow and scowled, "Ya think I don't know what that there word 'victuals' means don't you, but I got ya this time, Elvodug, you dummy."

"Yeah? What's it mean then?"

Flemup snickered, "Means when you went to the public privy."

Elvodug sneered back, "Well alright, I must've taught it to you before is all. You want to hear my news or what?"

"Guess so."

Elvodug was feeling important now, he could see that Flemup was trying to act uninterested, but he knew different. "I heard talk that the heroes won the day and beat those giants."

Flemup's eyes looked as if a big drop of cold rain just plopped down his collar. "You don't say! That's somethin'. How'd it come about?"

"Don't know. That's all I heard. Asked the fellow, but he turned his nose up at me and walked away."

"Aint that the way it always is."

"Yep, then I heard someone else sayin' how the witch Esla collapsed right there on the king's platform. She was in a bad way. By midnight she was dead … some kind a sickness." Elvodug spoke the last words with a knowing glint in his eyes.

Flemup returned the same look, nodding his head like he was the wisest of men. "We'll be safe," he whispered.

"You know it, we'll sure be safe." Elvodug agreed.

The two thieves opened one of the many small bags tied to their belts and took out a pinch of ash. Slowly they knelt down, scraped up some dirt and mixed it with the ash in the palm of their hands.

"Dog urine?" Flemup asked.

"Think we ought to … it's better to be safe." Elvodug uncorked a tiny vial and put a few drops in each of their hands. They smiled through yellow and black teeth as they rubbed the pungent concoction onto their skin. Elvodug and Flemup were of the decided opinion that the dirtier and smellier they were the safer they were from sickness.

"I got more news. Saw someone." Elvodug was suddenly serious. He didn't have to muster any special tone this time to stress the importance of his words; it just came natural, for the subject matter put a fear in him.

Flemup stopped eating, "What? Who?"

"Mortimer Blud!" Elvodug whispered, eyes darting in every direction just in case Mortimer was somewhere about.

"Oh! That is news! He's on the trail of someone then, and whoever it is doesn't have a chance."

"Scared?"

"Yep. Just glad he's not huntin' me. Hope I don't see him. You scared of him?"

"Yep. Gives me the shivers just thinkin' about him." Elvodug wasn't embarrassed by the admission — Mortimer Blud was just that plain frightening.

Flemup got very still and elbowed Elvodug. "Look at that, it's one of them children. The little one's leavin'."

Elvodug squinted his eyes. "You stay here, and keep your eyes open this time. I've got myself a hunt of my own to do."

The Candles

Percival had never stood inside a shop before. He had dreamed of what it would be like, and he'd seen people come out of them with packages of wonderful things; but he had never dared step foot in one, let alone purchase something. The only customer walked out just as Percival walked in.

He thought that surely the shop keeper would hear his heart thumping.

The man was a bit wide about the middle, his cheeks were wider still, and he hummed as he worked. He seemed a kindly person; Percival hoped so.

Percival stood before the counter. "Candle please, sir." His throat felt tight; not much of a sound came out.

The shop keeper looked about, astonished, "Who said that?"

"Me, sir, it's me. Down here." Percival squeaked again.

"I declare," the shop keeper said, alarmed, "we can't have beggars in here, sorry, you'll have to leave … quick now …"

Big tears threatened to ruin everything. Percival didn't want them to, and he was sure a knight wouldn't cry, but, for some reason, it was much harder to be brave here than it was in the face of a charging horse or a crazed mob.

The shop keeper's anxiety intensified. "That won't do … you see. I give you something out of the kindness of my heart, and then you'll be back every day, and every beggar in the city will be expecting a hand out … and my customers will be frightened off … you see how it is now don't you?"

Percival nodded his head, afraid to speak, for then he knew the tears would come. He turned away.

Suzie wouldn't get her candle. He failed his first quest; it was harder than he thought, being a knight and protector. But he wouldn't cry, at least he wouldn't do that.

Even that was proving quite difficult; his shoulders began to quake by the time he reached the door.

"Wait a minute," the shop keeper called. "What's that you're carrying?"

"My sword," Percival answered quietly, turning.

"Bring it here so I can see it better."

Percival held up the short stick he'd found in the tower's rubble. "I'm a knight."

The shop keeper's eyes lit up; they had gentleness and kindness in them. "A knight you say? And this is your sword?"

"Yep, hadn't had to use it yet. But I think I'll be pretty good with it."

"Of course … of course. What do you say if I purchase that sword from you?"

"Oh, I couldn't do that, sir. How will I protect my lady?"

The shop keeper smiled for the first time; Percival was won over completely. "I see your need, Mr. Shop Keeper," Percival began, "and I really want to help you, because that's what I do, but I've got a little lady that's needin' more help than you right now … cause you're a man and all. But as soon as I get a better sword, cause I suspect I'll eventually get a better one, then I'll just give this one to you as a gift. You'll not need to pay anything for it."

The shop keeper didn't seem to know what to say to that. He even looked like, well sort of like, he might cry. Maybe business hadn't been so good for him lately. A purchase might raise his spirits some.

"But, I can still help you, Mr. Shop keeper." Percival dug in his pocket and pulled out a copper. "Will this be enough to buy a candle?"

"It will, and then some," He said with a huskiness in his voice.

Percival smiled and placed the copper on the counter. "That's grand. I'll take one candle please, and you have the rest as a gift, Mr. Shop keeper."

It always came on sudden; that tickle in his chest. If only it wouldn't come now. The tickle rose up inside his lungs and no amount of holding his breath could stop it. Percival tried extra hard though, for he had seen people's reactions to his fits before; besides that, it didn't seem like something a knight would do.

The spasm was so strong when it came that he dropped his stick and fell to his knees. It hurt bad; he wheezed for breath and each cough felt like something was ripping apart in his lungs till there was no more air left to cough out, and then he would suck in with all his might, his breath wheezing and whistling to fill up his tiny lungs, but before he had sufficiently done so, the wracking cough would begin again.

He shut his eyes, struggling — he thought of Pip alone without him and Suzie waiting for her candle. He begged God to help him.

When he opened his eyes he was still alive, for the shop keeper was looming over him. Percival's breathing was easier but he felt very tired.

"I'm sorry, Mr. Shop keeper. I didn't mean to."

"Of course not … of course not — nothing to be sorry for. Here now, take this. Your copper has bought two candles and a pair of socks. Don't walk around outside with them or they'll wear out in a few days. But they'll keep your feet warm when you're sleeping or about your place. And if you find me a sword like yours, I'll trade you some of my goods for it.

"Remember, I'd not like a bunch of beggars in my shop. But you and I shall be friends. No one's come in here before and tried to give something to me … It's done my heart a good turn."

Percival stood on his toes and reached as high as he could, offering his hand. "My name's Pup, but Pip, he's my big brother, he says that's no name for a brave boy like me, so I'm called Percival, sir."

The shop keeper took Percival's hand gently in his. His hand was warm. "I'm Wig Magoon, you can call me Mr. Wig."

"Thank you, Mr. Wig. It's mighty fine havin' you for a friend. Thank you, sir."

Percival felt as if his heart had been done a good turn also.

He stepped out the door into the crowded street and immediately felt something was wrong. Though young, he'd had enough experiences with danger to develop a sense for it; a survival instinct that Pip had taught him how to use to his advantage — the weak must run and hide.

There was a terrible smell; something akin to sour milk and urine. It felt as though the smell itself was about to wrap its hands about him, enter his lungs, and finish him off right then and there.

Percival bolted under a slow moving carriage and grabbed onto its underbelly, clutching with his bare toes and fingers, he held on tight as the cobbles passed beneath him, his candle-carrying-socks clenched in his teeth. But he was not nearly as strong as Pip yet, and he couldn't hold on long.

Extending his arms until his back touched the cobbles, he let go, and rolled to the opposite side, jumped to his feet and immersed himself in the crowd.

He was almost home when he caught another whiff of that stench. It had come from before him, almost as if the smell knew where he was going and had cut him off. There were a few faces and arms and legs within the crowd that he was distrustful of, anyone of them could be the bearer of that smell. But they were fleeting glimpses, for he had it only in mind to escape.

Percival changed directions suddenly and made his way around the tower, to the alley, and into the grave-yard. He hid under a raised sarcophagus, trying to quiet his ragged breathing.

A footstep, then another not far away.

Percival's breathing was becoming more regular. He begged God to keep any coughing fits away.

The footsteps were getting closer, but he was well hid; Percival knew how to hide. Pip said he was uncommonly good at it.

Then the smell wafted into his hiding place. Percival held his breath to keep it out.

"Percival?" a voice said, not kindly, but not unkindly either.

"Percival, you might as well come out. I know you're here. I've come to help you."

Who could it be? How did he know his name? Was this stinky man sent from God? Percival wanted to know, but the feeling of danger was still there.

The voice continued, "I've come to help you with your candles. I'll make it so you don't have to buy another one, ever. Just think of what that would mean to your friends. A youngling like yourself carryin' more than his weight by supplyin' all the candles they'd ever need. You'd be Suzie's hero."

The voice knew about the candles and Suzie's name. Percival peeked out from one side of the sarcophagus, ready to roll out the other and run if need be. "Did Noah's God send you?"

The foul smelling man's looks matched his stench. He stood about ten feet from Percival's hiding place. He turned a yellow toothed smile towards the boy. "From God? No, not from him."

"How'd ya know my name then?" Percival asked.

"Magic." The man bowed majestically. "I am Elvo the wizard. You've heard of me, I'm sure?"*

Percival stared in awe. "No." His voice was little more than a whisper; he shrank back.

"Don't worry, boy," Elvo said, "I only practice good magic, none of the black arts for me ya understand. That's

---

* Note: Elvodug is not really a magician. Being only five years old and never having been taught our perfect and holy God's views concerning magic, Percival was thoroughly deceived, tossed to and fro by Elvodug, the pretend wizard and his doctrines of devils. See the scriptures on magic at the end of the book.

why I like to share the blessings of it with others. You see, if I find a person who's in need of the magic, then it comes back on me doubly good; the more in need you are the better for me. And you have the look of one in need."*

"I do?" Percival asked.

"The magic is practically begging me to help you. It's chosen you."

"Really?"

"Yes, you're one of the special ones."

"Oh, go figure. I didn't know that," Percival reflected. "I would've thought the magic would choose Suzie then. She's very special."

"Yes, indeed." Elvo's look became grave and mysterious. "The magic tells me that Suzie is safe, high up somewhere—"

Percival gasped, thinking of the tower.

"And I see Thiery and Pip, but they are not clear. They're fuzzy, they're in the tower with Suzie … No, they're not in the tower with Suzie … I can't be sure. The magic

---

*"But evil men and <u>seducers</u> shall wax worse and worse, <u>deceiving, and being deceived</u>. But continue thou in the things which thou hast learned and hast been assured of, knowing of whom thou hast learned them; And that **<u>from a child thou hast known the holy scriptures</u>**, which are **<u>able to make thee wise</u>** unto salvation through faith which is in Christ Jesus." 2 Timothy 3:13,14 "That we henceforth be no more children, tossed to and fro, and carried about with every wind of doctrine, <u>by the sleight of men, and cunning craftiness, whereby they lie in wait to deceive</u>." Ephesians 4:15

wants to tell us more, but it can't be sure …" Elvo gazed at Percival, a questioning, beckoning look upon his face.

"No, they won't be back till a lot after dark," Percival breathed, hoping he was of some help.

Elvo smiled his yellowed, rotting grin. "The magic is very pleased, see, it knew you were special. It seems then she is alone, and you will be her guardian and hero then. You will be a great hero to keep her safe—"

"And Horatio will help me," Percival interrupted, feeling a little embarrassed with so much praise all for himself.

The wizard Elvo looked startled. "Horatio?"

"He's a great big wolf. Even a giant wolf. Not as big as God, He's the biggest." Percival widened his arms as far as they would go, then he made a snarling face. "And Horatio will eat anyone that tries to get at Suzie. Of course, my sword is dangerous too."

Elvo's eyes were suddenly very big. He shrank back.

"Oh, I'm very sorry," Percival blurted. "I didn't mean to scare you."

"A wolf you say? A real, live wolf?"

"Yes. Horatio, and he can tell bad men from good men just like that. Probably could swallow them whole … hmmm … maybe not whole."

The magician seemed to have lost his eagerness. He was quiet for a while. He paced, scratched his dirty beard, and almost spoke a time or two. Then all at once the light in his eyes surged back. "Percival! That's it! The wolf is the key.

"Put one of your candles at the base of this grave marker. Then come back with your wolf as soon as it is dark. Walk him around the grave yard ten times … then bring him to the candle … then start scratching his ears and all the places your wolf likes to be scratched. I don't know how long it will take, but your candle will soon turn into two, then three, then four and so on right before your eyes. It will be a rare thing, but you will be one of the special ones to witness it.

"Can you remember what to do?" Elvo asked with wonder in his voice.

Percival was too amazed to speak. He nodded his head.

"Good. Just one more thing – don't mention me or it won't work. Never mention the wizard until the magic has run its course."

Percival nodded. This was too amazing, too exciting. It was just like some of the stories that Pip had told him, only now, Percival was the hero, the special one, and he was going to see real magic happen right before his eyes.

But something felt funny inside and it was almost as if a still, small voice, whispered, "Beware."

A Sick Visitor

Elvodug looked suspiciously at Flemup. Flemup looked guiltily back.

"You look like you've just woken up." Elvodug growled. He began to shake with anger.

"Sleep? Me?" Flemup tried hard to look innocent of the charge, but in his grogginess he couldn't keep back a yawn.

Elvodug's eyes narrowed to slits.

"Okay, maybe I did, maybe I didn't. But you fed me that costly greasy food. It made me tired. A man can't be expected to fill his belly and then just stare wide eyed at nothin' for as long as you've been gone. Nothin's happened and it makes a man tired to watch nothin'.

"Anyway, I think my eyes just closed seconds before you arrived, and now that you're here I'll let them take the course they've been waitin' to take."

Without another word, Flemup laid down and promptly fell asleep.

Elvodug wondered how he'd put up with such buffoonery for all these years. Maybe one day he'd get another partner … but old habits were hard to break, and Flemup felt like an old habit.

Still, since Elvodug was the mastermind behind all their first-rate schemes, then maybe he ought to at least get a bigger share of their earnings.

The thought was a good one; shocking really, that he hadn't realized it earlier. Just look at the way he'd handled that little Percival. Flemup could never have pulled off such a performance.

Elvodug didn't even mind that Flemup was sleeping, for he awaited dusk with great pleasure — pleasure to see his plan work so flawlessly, and an even greater pleasure to see Flemup's amazement when he comprehended the extent of Elvodug's genius.

When Percival entered in through the secret door, Horatio wasn't there to meet him. Either he was getting better at sneaking about on quiet feet, or Horatio was kept busy by something above, maybe something dangerous — Percival drew his stick and primed himself for battle. This involved a narrowing of the eyes, a grim setting of the teeth, and of course, a prayer to Noah's God to make him brave.

Half way up the stairs, and still there was no Horatio to meet him. It was quiet up there.

He knew that the next three stairs all squeaked, and there was no way with his little legs that he could step over them.

He had already tried every spot upon the steps when working on his sneaking skills, and even Pip hadn't been able to manage their passing without some noise.

He rushed up them, imagining himself to be an acrobat; the second his foot touched a tread, he instantly removed it, so as to pass up them like a flying thing. It was his best try yet, but still the second stair gave a groaning protest at being stepped upon.

Percival froze, peered up at the corner of the doorway, and waited.

Pad, pad, pad.

It sounded like the wolf approaching.

Pad, pad, pad.

Horatio's big head appeared at the entrance, ears at attention. Now, the big wolf would joyously clamber down the stairs to greet Percival — but he did not. Horatio only glanced at Percival and padded back into the room.

It was strange behavior.

Percival decided it would be best to keep himself guarded and ready. There didn't seem to be any danger, but Pip always said that the moment you let your guard slip, that's when you're most at risk; and Horatio's behavior was strange.

But he was not prepared for the scene that met him as he slipped into the upper chamber. Suzie was on her knees before Gimcrack's cot, dabbing the forehead of a man with a wet cloth. Horatio was almost knocking her over as he pressed close against her.

The man was much too big to be Gimcrack.

Percival came closer and gasped when he saw the face. The eyes were closed, with dark circles beneath them, and the skin was pale and waxy, but it was definitely him.

"That's the man," Percival said, bewildered. "He's the one God sent to help me in the streets, and who gave us all that food."

Suzie turned, her voice filled with hope, "Really, Percival? You're sure it was him?"

"I wouldn't forget a thing like that." Percival said.

"Oh … then it is too wonderful, just too wonderful," she whispered.

Percival thought so too, but he felt like he was missing something.

"You see," Suzie began, excitedly, "this is Count Rosencross, who sent me away to keep the Dragon Priests from getting me."

"Ohhhh," Percival said, drawing the word out to show just how amazed he was.

"Yes, and I think that God has been calling very clearly to him, and he has done very bad things, and so he cannot see a way to come to Him, or maybe he still wants to follow false gods, and his conscience is bearing witness against him.

"I think God has surely brought him to us, and in a humbled state, so that maybe he will turn to the one true God with all his heart and mind and soul.

"After you left I heard something fall down on the roof. Horatio and I went to see what it was, and it was him, weak as a baby. Let us love him as God loves us, Percival."

Percival and Suzie started at the same moment. The Count's eyes were open, feverishly bright. Just as suddenly they closed. He seemed to put forth a great effort. They slowly opened a crack, and then they fell shut; his head lolled to the side. His was not a peaceful sleep; his brow furrowed, groans escaped his lips, and soon his face was flushed.

"Will he die?" Percival asked after a while.

"I don't think so. He's very strong."

"Yes, I think he must be." Percival studied the Count's face to make sure he was really asleep, and then asked the question that was bothering him. "What bad things has he done, Suzie?"

"He worships Marduk instead of the God of Noah. He's a man stealer; I saw him do it once … it was horrible. He's brought the evil priests of the Dragon with him, who practice magic and other such terrible things. And I don't know what else, but isn't it wonderful that despite all of that, God still would have him as His own, if he would only repent and run into His arms? And when I've sung to him about our God, I've seen him soften, and I've seen the battle for his soul raging across his face, just as plain as can be."

At the mentioning of magic, something pricked Percival on the insides. What was that uncomfortable feeling? He tried to shrug it off.

"How do you know so much, Suzie?"

"It's only because God was so graceful and merciful that, seeing me in my need, He sent an old woman at the end of her life, to pour into me the truth and love of God. She was my nurse-maid for two years. Her name was Lois, Grandmother Lois is what I called her. She had an amazing faith that dwelt in her, and I am persuaded that, through her diligence, she has passed it on to me."

The feeling on his insides was getting worse. "Suzie?"

"Yes, Percival, what is it?"

"You said somethin' about magic. I suppose you were talkin' about black magic … did Grandmother Lois ever say anything about that?" Percival looked down at the ground as he said it.

"Oh my, yes. At least three or four times a week she warned me, 'cause it's all around us — sorceries, astrologers, enchantments, familiar spirits, those that seek after wizards, to be defiled by them, witches, and charmers — and it can be very sneaky."

"What d'ya mean, sneaky?" Percival's heart was pounding now.

"Well, Satan likes to make evil things look good so that we'll be more likely to pursue them, and in so doing we disobey God and wander away from Him. Woe to them that call evil good, and good evil."

"Makes them look good? How does he do that?" Percival asked.

"Well, like in the Garden, God told Adam and Eve that they would surely die in the day that they ate of the tree of the knowledge of good and evil. Satan came to Eve and told her that she would not surely die; that her eyes would be opened, and she would be as a god."

"Oh no! That's awful. She didn't fall for it though, right?"

"I'm afraid she did."

Percival gasped. "But how could she disobey something so clear?"

"Because she saw that the tree was good for food, and that it was pleasant to the eyes, and a tree to be desired to make one wise. And she was deceived."

"I hope I never disobey God for any reason at all!" Percival said at length, and then hesitated before he went on speaking, "and what about magic?"

"That's right, I forgot. Well, God says that the soul that turns after such as have familiar spirits, and after wizards …. He says, 'I will even set my face against that soul, and will cut him off from among his people'. He says of the enchanters, witches, wizards and others who practice magic; all that do these things are an abomination unto the Lord.

"See, Grandmother Lois used to say that magic is like Satan's imitation of God's wondrous power. If we want to know the future, or see one loaf of bread turned into many, or any other wonders that man can not normally do, then it is only okay to seek for such things directly through God himself. Whether or not He does them is completely up to Him, as He sees fit. But trying to make those things happen ourselves — magic — is to make ourselves like God."

"But, if someone were going to use magic to make an extra loaf of bread, so that they could give it to someone, isn't that good magic?" Percival asked.

"No, it is disobedience; because God said not to do it at all. Remember, how Eve came up with seemingly good reasons to disobey God, and you thought it a terrible thing. See now, how one can be led astray from God's commandments. Grandma Lois called it our itching ears. Some things are easy for certain people to obey, yet hard for others, because their itching ear, their desire, wants the thing so badly, they'll listen to any argument that allows them to have it. While others don't care so much, so they find that same commandment easier to obey. A keeper of God's word is one who wants to obey everything God says no matter what."

"I see it now. I've always loved the magic stories that Pip used to tell me, and so I didn't want to believe that they were bad. I want to be a Keeper of God's word though … I won't let my ear itch about it anymore … only … I hope Pip won't be mad at me. And …" Percival almost told Suzie about Elvo the Wizard when he was startled again by Count Rosencross' wide open eyes.

How long had he been watching them and listening? Would he be angry at their talk?

The Count looked from one to the other of the children.

"Water …" he said with an effort; his tone was even.

He drank a whole cupful. It seemed that he might have smiled feebly at them, though it could have been a grimace.

Then, his eyes were closed, and his breathing steady.

After Dark

The sun set, bathing the city in shadowy dark. Count Rosencross had slept through the day. Thiery and Pip had still not returned. Suzie lit their only candle and smiled at Percival.

"Thank you," she said. "It makes me feel so nice, especially now that it's dark."

Percival felt cheerful all over again.

Horatio walked over to the stairway and looked back at them. The wolf's eyes met Percival's, he gave a low whine, and then turned his head to look down the stairs.

"I think he has to go potty," Suzie said. "What if Thiery and Pip don't get back till late?"

"I'll walk him," Percival said, hopefully. "Thiery showed me how to put his saddle on, and you've seen how good I can turn him."

Gimcrack had made Horatio a wolf saddle out of some riding equipment found among the Dwarven Brotherhood's things, and Percival would rather have been on Horatio's back than anywhere else in the world.

"I don't know." Suzie looked worried.

"Thiery says I'm a natural at it, and I know just where to walk him."

Suzie nibbled at her bottom lip.

Percival's expression pleaded for Suzie's permission. It would be a great adventure to ride proudly upon the back of his giant wolf-steed; just like a real knight, and he just knew that Suzie would be greatly impressed by it.

"I've got an idea," Percival said, at last. "You can stand here at the window, holdin' the candle. It looks down on the grave-yard. That way you can see me and I can look up and see you. Won't that be pleasant? We'll both know that the other one is safe."

In the end, Horatio decided the matter by his increased prancing and whining. He even knocked little Percival over twice while he strapped and buckled the harnesses in place; Percival thought it was great fun and only giggled until he saw the concern clouding Suzie's face.

He gave Horatio the command to lay down with as serious a tone as he could muster. Horatio obeyed, but the excitement to get going was bottled up something fierce. Percival now had his new jacket, socks, and boots on, and his sword-stick was sheathed in the saddle; he sure felt like a grown up knight; his grin was beginning to hurt.

Percival looked at Suzie out of the corner of his eye; she was all attention.

He jumped into the saddle and then they were speeding down the stairs. There was no time to give the right kind of goodbye, he had planned to say something grand, but Horatio just took off; well, he could make up for it by giving a good speech when he got back. If only Pip and Thiery could be there, and if the Count woke up, then Suzie would really think it was something to have all of them just listening to Percival's tales of brave adventure.

Horatio made straight for the grave-yard. Percival didn't try to give him any directions yet, Horatio was too intent upon doing his business after spending all day inside.

There was Suzie, way up in the tower, and a tiny glow from the candle — the candle! In all the excitement he had forgotten that the second candle was out here, and he was supposed to do that magic stuff to make it turn into a whole bunch of them.

Don't worry God, Percival prayed, *I won't do any magic, not at all, not one bit. I want to be a keeper of your Word like Suzie said, and I don't want to have itchy ears either.*

Then it struck him that maybe Elvo the wizard was out here too. He sure had smelled bad; he didn't have a very nice look about him either. Percival remembered that his first instincts had been to run from the man, and even after they had spoken for awhile, he still hadn't felt comfortable getting too close.

Percival glanced up at Suzie; the candle was still burning, but he had difficulty seeing her from where he was. Percival clicked his tongue to the roof of his mouth, just as Thiery had taught him, and Horatio responded by moving forward.

Pressing with his knees, Percival guided the wolf among the graves, away from the tower so as to increase his visibility of the illuminated window-slit.

Suzie wasn't there. Why had she moved? Perhaps Count Rosencross had needed something; but Percival felt a growing uneasiness.

An image of Elvo the wizard with his rotting, yellowed smile sprang into his mind. It was an eerie thing to recall while in the midst of a grave-yard, even if Horatio was with him. Elvo had only smiled once. It was like a smile of triumph. He had done it right after Percival told him that Suzie was alone in the tower.

Percival tried to think. It seemed he was on to something, but what? What else had Elvo the wizard said? That's right — he had said that the wolf was the key … that Horatio was the key. What did that mean?

Then Elvo told him to bring Horatio out here right after dark. Which he had. It suddenly made a terrifying kind of sense. That would mean both of Suzie's protectors, Percival and Horatio, would be out of the way, unable to help poor Suzie.

Hadn't Thiery mentioned something about two thieves who had pretended to be Suzie's uncles? Something about their smell — a stink no one would ever forget no matter how much one wanted to.

Percival felt sick all of a sudden; sick with fear — fear for Suzie.

Something moved upon the tower's rooftop and then was gone.

"Horatio!" Something in the little boy's tone caused the wolf to go rigid. Percival could feel the deep guttural growl pulsing against his knees. "To Suzie, Horatio, to Suzie!"

Horatio flew through the grave-yard, bounding amongst the graves and dark gaping holes in the earth, like the hunter giving chase amongst the trees, stretching out its gait with the eager hope to pull down its prey — Percival held tight, the air whipping through his hair. They must get to Suzie in time.

Horatio was a wild wolf once again, intent upon one thing — finding the danger that threatened the little boy upon his back and the little girl within their stony lair, and destroy it.

As Percival pressed the catch to open the secret door at the base of the tower, he heard voices above. It caused him to pause and consider. Yes, he and Horatio would sneak up the stairs quickly but quietly, so as to take them by surprise. Pip had taught him over and over the importance of surprise.

He recognized the first voice as that of Count Rosencross. "How dare you, Priest!" He was furious, but weak.

The second voice must have been the priests'. "I dare, because the Dragon has claimed her." The priest's voice sounded like his nose was pinched, and he spoke with arrogance and a commanding tone that even Percival knew was not appropriate to use when addressing the Count.

"You will order those putrid thieves to bring her back at once." It sounded like the Count was struggling to rise to his feet.

"I'm afraid, that even I could not catch them right now," the priest said. "You gave them quite a scare. We did not expect to find you here, Count. In any event you can do nothing in your condition to stop us, and I will not obey you over the Dragon."

"Then I will kill you when next we meet!" Rosencross growled.

The priest laughed mockingly. "You would have done better had you kept that to yourself, Count. I don't think it wise for there to be a next time. We could have done so much, you and I. But you've let those children poison your mind. The Dragon promised you power and wealth beyond imagination and what do you do? You try to stay my hand concerning my own children—"

"They are not your children!" The Count declared, raising his voice. "They are mine! I'll not lose any more to you or the Dragon."

Percival heard a hiss of surprise or anger or both. "Your sickness has made you mad!" The priest shrieked. "It is I who will kill you!"

Percival drew his stick-sword and yelled, "Charge!"

The candle was far away from where the Count and priest argued — it was a terrible place of darkness. Worse yet, a breeze threatened the small flame so that it danced and sputtered making a myriad of shifting shadows play across them so that it seemed to Percival almost as if the two men were only one.

Exactly what happened next, Percival couldn't tell.

The Count cried out as if struck by a blow and fell to the floor.

The shadows continued to flit and rise and fall. And Percival stared into the recesses of the room in vain. He could not see the priest anywhere. He was gone. The smell of Elvo the Wizard still clung to the room; Horatio growled as he checked every corner. But there was no priest, no thieves, no wizard, and no Suzie.

Count Rosencross was still breathing, but he was unconscious or asleep. There was no wound that Percival could see. He could not wake him, though he tried desperately.

"Suzie?" Percival called pitifully. "Suzie, are you hiding? Suzie?"

He had failed her. He had failed in his duty to protect his favorite friend.

Where was Pip? Where was Thiery?

Please God let them come home right now. I don't know what to do.

Horatio whined and licked Percival's cheek.

Hungry Badgers

Only an hour earlier, Mamma, the giant badger, had nudged and prodded her three skunks; for she considered them her own little ones.

Of them all, they had the most boldness with the man-things, in fact they were the first to accept her own adopted man-thing. The young wolverines had been the last to accept him, and even then it was with reluctance. Lately they seemed to be having trouble even with each other, and then yesterday they had come and touched Mamma's nose with their own, and padded away in opposite directions.

It was their leave-taking. Wolverines are solitary creatures, and these two were almost fully grown, so that their instinct to have their own territory had emerged too strong to ignore any longer.

Mamma had a deep sadness that she could not shake; it made her feel sluggish and tired.

First she had buried one of the fox kits which had fallen in an accident; then she had lost the man-thing in the battle with the bright-shinies; then her only remaining fox kit was taken by a panther—she had been too weak and sick to do anything about it; and now her skunks would not move or wake.

They had gone into their time of the deep-sleep. She knew that they would wake once in a while throughout the winter months, but it did not help. All of her adopted ones were gone to her, in one way or another, and the sadness remained.

The other badgers, six of them, had all survived the battle of the bright-shinies and they looked to her now with hunger in their bellies. Mamma felt the stirrings of it herself. She left her sleeping skunks reluctantly; if only the man-thing was here to bring her another young cub or kit to nuzzle and care for.

Emerging from two of the den's runs, they sniffed the ground and air, cautiously looking for any sign of danger.

Hunger compelled them to the hunt.

They had not visited the place of many smells for over a week. It was at the outskirts of their hunting grounds, and very close to the giant den of the man-things. Instinctively, they knew it was a place of great danger, but still it enticed them to visit often; all those unusual smells and foods that tasted nothing like what they were used to — Mamma could almost taste the treats already, and having thought of it, she began to feel a little better.

The sun was well set when the badger clan arrived to begin their scrounging and feasting.

The smelling place was a refuse pile, not of human waste, but a dumping ground for the city of Hradcanny, of which food, no longer good for human consumption, was thrown into a massive heap from the towering northern wall. The mountains were to the north of the city, and so Strongbow had let the woods grow and creep closer on that side, effectively giving the animals a feeling of security as they approached.

It did not take long to fill their bellies. Mamma waited as the last of the badgers were finishing. Something moved at the top of the wall — man-things.

She gave the warning, and the clan melted back into the edge of the wood. A moment later and a great bag descended; by what means, Mamma could not comprehend. The only things she had ever seen in the air were birds and the occasional dragon-kind, and this was neither.

She caught a whiff that made her fear a little, but then she heard a sound coming from the bag, a small sound, a young sound, and her badger heart longed to help it and snuggle against it.

In a moment, she was at the thing's side. There was a long rope attached to the bag, the other end hung from the big wall. She had never dared come this close to the wall before, and the fear came upon her much stronger now. A man-paw showed itself over the wall's top, and then a face.

The fear almost won out, and Mamma almost ran for the safety of the wood. But then one of the pitiful sounds issued forth from the bag, inflaming the giant badger's heart to courage. The young one needed protecting. With that thought, Mamma felt ten times stronger and ten times more courageous.

In an instant she chewed through the rope with her sharp teeth and powerful jaws.

She sniffed the bag. The little thing inside went still. Mamma could smell the poor creature's fear, and other smells too that she would store away in her mind, ready to call them up again if needed, for she did not like them. She felt that the ones who had made those smells were also the ones who had caused the fear in the little one. It made her angry.

Mamma bit gently into the top of the bag where the rope had been tied. She lifted the burden, scrambled across the heap, and disappeared into the forest with her clan.

A clan that was now increased by one.

And that one needed her care and protection.

The sadness lifted from Mamma's heart.

The Council

"What's happening?" Thiery asked, as the bells in New City rang out — two short clangs followed by a long deep one. The hustle of the streets stopped for a moment; people tilted their heads as they listened.

"A high council is being called," Pip answered. "And if we don't hurry we'll lose the better part of our day forced to watchin' it … ugh, too late."

City guards appeared from an alley not ten paces away and started driving those before them towards the sounding bells. "Council trial!" They proclaimed. "Theatre-in-the-round … move forward … you there, keep moving … to the amphitheatre with you … no excuses, everyone must go …" on and on the guards prodded the people caught within their net, until they rounded the corner of Warbling Street.

The narrow lane gave way to a wide open space, a rare sight within Old City. A number of steep swerving streets emptied into this place in a sort of irregular circle; guards herded men, women and children into it from all directions. There was a view all the way down to the port, and further up the hill one could see the Citadel's formidable walls, hovering over them.

Long ago, workers had cut into the hillside and carved out a stony amphitheatre. There were thirty rows of stone benches rising upward in a half circle. Many of those ushered in, knew the routine and they began to fill the benches. Thiery and Pip were seated in the first row. One of the guards came over and sat beside Thiery.

Before them was a slightly raised stage. The high-judgment seat was in the middle, two lesser-judgment seats on either side, collectively they were known as the council.

"Those are the judges," Pip said, pointing at the men upon the seats. "I've been made to watch one of these before. Took all day, and Master Squilby was fearsome mad with me. He said I should've snuck away from the dim-witted …" Pip's voice trailed off.

The guard looked over at them. He had a hard, weathered face. Both boys grew still before his gaze. "Dim-witted guards? Was that what you were about to say?"

Pip had the look of a wild animal about him, suddenly attentive to danger and ready to bolt at any sign of the predator's first move.

The guard laughed. "You've nothing to fear from me. I'm not in the habit of thrashing young boys."

The guard's face softened some now that it had given way to a smile, but Thiery could see confidence and strength in it that cautioned a person to tread carefully. He looked as if he could stare down the king himself if he had a mind to. "Your Master Squilby might be right, about some of us anyway. He ought to teach you to be more careful though with what you say, and before whom you say it."

"Yes, sir," Pip blurted, "you're very right, sir. It's the very thing he's always tellin' me, sir, or at least, he used to tell me. I'm sorry 'bout calling you dim-witted, I didn't mean to. I can tell you aren't in the least, dim-witted I mean."

The guard looked amused, but said no more.

Most of the citizens were now seated. A group of merchants had congregated at the edge of the stage, leaning with great attention towards the council.

The high-judgment seat was brimming over with a robed and gelatinous man; his flabby cheeks hung down into the rolling folds of his neck; he seemed to have no chin, and his eyes squinted like two raisins submerged in a bowl of pudding.

He turned his attention to the merchants and waved his hand in a slow beckoning fashion. One of their number scurried over to the foot of the high-counselor and bowed, begging permission for the merchants to sell food and drink; he emphasized their heartfelt desire to supply the counselors themselves with whatever they might need throughout the day, as a gift of course, from the members of the merchant's guild.

The high-counselor gave his assent without a word; a slight inclining of the head, and a flourish of his hand; the merchant bowed deeper still with much thanks and obeisance.

Theiry had much to say to Pip — intrigued by the proceedings — but he felt the guard's presence and was afraid to speak. Pip was uncommonly quiet.

It was the guard who spoke first.

In due course they learned his name and somewhat about him — he was Clum. Two years earlier, he had been Captain Clum, captain over a hundred men, and he had every intention of rising further. But that was not to be, for a wanted man had escaped his keeping. He was demoted to that of city guard, captain of no one but himself.

"But at least I can sleep at night, and look my wife and children in the eyes, for I did not shirk my duty." Clum winked at the boys. "Never shirk your duty whatever the cost." Then he sighed. "That is why I'm here today.

"I've another duty to carry out. In a moment you'll see a strange sight. I had my self transferred here this morning so I could be witness to it. Do you know what a Synod Horrenda is? Or maybe you've heard of it as a Cadaver Synod?"

Pip looked like he might bolt again.

"I see you do," Clum said to Pip. He turned his intense stare upon Thiery. "But you're still in the dark. Sometimes, a man so offends a lord or the king, that they hunt him down and destroy him, and that not being satisfactory, they exhume the body and put him on trial.

"I've only seen one, and I'd rather not see another. But the man they're putting on trial today helped me once when I was down, and I'd not sleep well if I didn't come. See that gaping hole in the hill behind us … that's where they'll bring him out. Only, I've been told he'll be walking on his own two feet, just as Lord McDougal did yesterday in the games; 'dead no more' is what they call him now."

Thiery could hardly believe what he was hearing. Lord McDougal … alive?

It must have shown on his face for Clum looked surprised. "Have you not heard what has happened at the games?"

"No, Captain Clum, we've heard nothing," Thiery said. "Would you be so kind to tell us?"

Clum seemed pleased to be called captain.

It would take some time for the merchants to sell their wares, and Clum settled down to tell the tale. He told them of the heroes who fought and vanquished the giants: Lord McDougal, Fergus Leatherhead, Igi Forkbeard, Blagger, who had died from his wounds, Count Rosencross, Oded 'the Bear', his brother Ubaldo 'the Silent', who they said would yet recover from his injuries, and Gimcrack the dwarf. The dwarf was also hurt, but as yet no one knew how bad, for the Dwarven Brotherhood appeared out of nowhere and stole him away, taking him somewhere beneath the city. The king had not liked that.

The heroes fought valiantly, all for the cause of Lady Mercy and the honor of the kingdom. The giants had been disgraced.

The city had never seen such games before. Strongbow received adoration from the crowds; they threw flowers upon his dais, and many said that there was never a king like him, that he was like a god. The king did like that.

Clum leaned in close to the boys and whispered, "Some of the guards say that the king is here right now, secretly watching, and it is true that we've been given special command to keep everything in perfect order; so perhaps he is. Look over there, a score of his best town criers and two of the king's personal scribes. If he's not here, he'll know every word that's spoken."

Thiery's head was spinning with so much news. Now he knew why Gimcrack had not returned. He prayed that God would keep him safe.

Lord McDougal was alive! Thinking of Suzie, he smiled.

And Oded was here, in the city; his heart felt great joy when he thought of seeing Oded again; for he had raised Thiery, and taught him many things; especially to love God with a simple and steadfast faith.

He wondered about Count Rosencross too; he had been there, with Thiery's father, the day Thiery lay sick within his tent. The Count had not seemed pleased with … with … what Thiery's father had done. Maybe Thiery could speak with the Count and find out more. Suzie liked him.

The merchants melted away.

The citizens, no more than a few hundred, were hushed and expectant. Very few had begun eating their foodstuffs; all eyes were upon the high-counselor.

His corpulent robe jiggled as he moved. It seemed that moving one part of his body would cause another part to respond, very much like a peat bog rippling when one stepped upon it, the fluid slime beneath its surface trying to emerge somewhere else.

The high-counselor raised his hand; there was complete silence.

"Come forth!" he commanded, with a very important and regal air. His neck undulated with the effort.

Nothing happened.

He leaned forward in his seat. The dark hole at the base of the amphitheatre stared back, empty, expressionless, undaunted by the high-counselor's command.

Sitting as close as he was, Thiery could see perspiration break out on the high-counselor's forehead.

He lifted his hand again. It shook ever so slightly.

There was a tinge of fear in his voice now.

"Staffsmitten, by the laws of the land and by commandment of the king himself, come forth to your trial!"

Synodus Horrenda

Staffsmitten walked stiffly from the dark tunnel. The crowd gasped; most people sitting close, leaned away from him as he passed; some leaned in for a better look.

It was to be a pretend 'Cadaver Synod' then — for Thiery knew that Staffsmitten had not really died. This was Gimcrack's friend, who had fought alongside Lord McDougal in the Death Hunt; who was keeper of the Dwarven Lesser Gate; and who had most likely trained Horatio, or at least begun his training.

These were strange days indeed. Thiery's mind raced with thoughts of what it all might mean. Only God could raise the dead. Yet someone wanted the citizens of Hradcanny to believe that Staffsmitten and Lord McDougal had died and then been raised to life, and Thiery was sure they hadn't gone to all this trouble hoping to draw souls to the one true God.

If nothing else, it excited the populace; there was a tangible thrill in the air, upon their faces, and in their whispering chatter. It gave Thiery an uneasy feeling. He heard someone behind him speaking to his neighbor. "The king has done what his father could not do … he's found the secrets of death and life. Strongbow himself might be one of the gods!"

Thiery shuddered. How any man could think he was a god seemed not only absurd but a terrible and fearful thing to contemplate.

The buzzing voices stopped as the high-counselor spoke; they dared not miss a word.

"Staffsmitten, son of Adelwolf?"

"It is I, Your Honor." Staffsmitten bowed slightly.

"You have been summoned by the king for a Synodus Horrenda. Can you speak for yourself, or shall we appoint a priest to give answers for you, as is the customary way?"

"I can speak for myself, Your Honor, for I am not dead, nor was I dead, and therefore this is not a Synodus—"

"Yes, yes, I understand the delusions of those who have traveled beyond the veil, Lord McDougal said the same." The high-counselor was annoyed. "We shall hear no more on that account, or a priest will answer for you. Is that understood?"

"Yes, Your Honor, perfectly well."

"Good. Staffsmitten, you are on trial, a Synodus Horrenda," the high-counselor said, stressing the last words, "for treason against the king, and against Hradcanny. How do you plead?"

"Innocent."

The high-counselor straightened his heaving girth as much as possible and scowled. "We shall see." Then turning to the scribes, he said, "I want it recorded that Staffsmitten neglected to call me 'Your Honor'. Did you not observe it my judges?"

"We did! We did! Most disrespectful! Most alarming! Rebellious!" The four judges piped from their lesser judgment seats, like four little birds opening their beaks in frenzied twitter whenever mother bird returned to the nest.

The high-counselor condescended to smile upon his doting judges.

It occurred to Thiery that this would not be the fairest of trials.

"Staffsmitten, did you or did you not aid Lord McDougal and his party on the night of the Death Hunt?"

"I did, Your Honor, but I see no treason against Hradcanny or the king, for I was already outside the city walls at the clanging of the bells. It could just have well been me that the Death Riders and hyenae were hunting. Why should I not then help Lord McDougal, who is also one of Hradcanny's defenders and one of the kingdom's lords."

The crowd murmured its approval at this defense.

The high-counselor's face reddened. "Call forth the witness, bring me Master Squilby."

There was a loud clattering of plates crashing to the ground, followed by angry shouts where the merchants had set up their food-stuffs. All eyes turned at the commotion.

When they turned back only a second later, Master Squilby was there, standing at attention before the judgment-seats.

It had its effect upon the people. For, Squilby was a name used to put fear into the hearts of young children when they would not obey their parents. Squilby, the evil dwarf, who rode through the sky with a flying creature; Squilby, who appeared as if out of thin air and lurked in shadows; Squilby, master of the sneaks, master of the hunt, and master of terrible beasts. Yes, parents told tales of Squilby that made their children tremble, but the name evoked such fear because the parents themselves trembled when they used it.

"Master Squilby?"

"It is I, Your Honor." Squilby bowed deeply.

"Master Squilby, you were out the night of the last hunt?"

"Yes, Your Honor."

"You, were in fact, on the ground, in the woods when Staffsmitten and Lord McDougal's party came together?"

"I was, Your Honor."

"And you overheard their conversation?"

"I did, Your Honor."

The high-counselor gloated over each word. "Tell us then, what passed between them."

"Yes, Your Honor. Staffsmitten told Lord McDougal that the Chronicler's ship was waiting for them near Knucker's Pool."

"Aha!" the high-counselor cried, trying to raise himself from his seat and then giving up. "Did you hear that, judges?"

"We did! We did! Most condemning! Terrible! Treasonous!" The judges blurted.

"Call the second witness." The high-counselor was working himself into an agitated state, his hand waved almost absentmindedly at his side as if to hurry the witness along. "Chronicler, we call you to witness against this man and against yourself."

Two guards came forward with a man between them, slight of build, impeccably dressed, with black hair and a long twisted mustache.

The guards hesitated before the high-counselor's glare. "I said, the Chronicler. What is wrong with your ears?"

Before the guards could find their tongues, the man between them bowed. "I am Diego Dandolo, Your Honor, assistant to the Chronicler. He has sent me on his behalf."

"On his behalf!" the high-counselor's beady eyes looked like they might pop from his head in astonishment.

"If I may explain, Your Honor," Diego bowed again. "The Chronicler was served this morning with a request for his appearance here, and as he was very busy, and as you know he is quite old, he deemed it reasonable to send me in his stead. If he had known what this was about, that Staffsmitten was on trial, and that you would accuse him of treason then he most certainly would have come in person. Would you like me to go and get him?"

The high-counselor's eyes receded back to their narrowed slits; his face and neck were now covered with red blotches. "No, you shall not 'go and get him'. This is a trial. Scribes, make note that the Chronicler has disregarded his summons to the council. His guilt being well established by his own actions and the words of Master Squilby. I think we have enough to pass judgment, but I will press it a little further.

"Diego Dandolo, can you tell us if the Chronicler was inside the city or outside the city on the night of the hunt?"

"Yes, Your Honor, he and I were inside the city," Diego said, and then added. "The Chronicler was the special guest of King Strongbow. He and the king are good friends you know, long time friends."

"There you have it! Inside the city! Two witnesses against him."

"If I may, Your Honor," Diego said, bowing again, "but I shall never be 'against' the Chronicler — though it is quite apparent that you are. The king has always been *for* the Chronicler, the people of Hradcanny have always been *for* the Chronicler. I dare even say that the people love him. Yet you are clearly *against* him. You are not on trial, so I shall not ask you why."

The crowd's suspicions were piqued — it did seem that this council was predetermined to find Staffsmitten and the

Chronicler guilty. The high-counselor was an important man, but who was he when compared to the Chronicler.

The high-counselor looked alarmed. "Of course, of course, the Chronicler is well loved," he said, acquiescing before the people. "It is only truth for which I dig. I shall proceed with greater care.

"Tell me, Diego Dandolo, what gods does the Chronicler worship?"

Diego hesitated.

"Surely," the high-counselor raised his voice, "being his assistant, you can give us an answer."

"He worships the God of Noah, Your Honor."

"And what others?"

"No others, as is well understood by most of Hradcanny."

"I see," the high-counselor smiled coldly. "He holds that the god of Noah is the one true god? Is that not how you people put it?"

"Yes, Your Honor."

"And the gods that the rest of us worship," the high-counselor waved his hand towards the crowd, "they are not real gods at all?"

"That's right, Your Honor."

The high-counselor had quickly and deftly placed the populace back on his side. He no longer looked alarmed, but triumphant. Next, he brought out a slew of witnesses, students and peers of the Chronicler's, who had much to say against him, though Thiery found himself greatly admiring the boldness by which the Chronicler had testified to them about his God.

Their witness against the Chronicler turned many hearts in the amphitheatre from annoyance to anger to vehemence: 'We ought not to think that the Godhead is like unto gold, or silver, or stone, graven by art and man's device.' 'They shall be ashamed, and also confounded, all of them: they shall go to confusion together that are makers of idols.' 'They have no knowledge that set up the wood of their graven image, and pray unto a god that cannot save.' 'And there is no God else beside me; a just God and a Saviour; there is none beside me. Look unto me, and be ye saved, all the ends of the earth: for I am God, and there is none else.' 'Surely, shall one say, In the Lord have I righteousness and strength: even to him shall men come; and all that are incensed against him shall be ashamed.'

And many other such testimony was heard until a riot seemed imminent, people jumped to their feet as the last of the witnesses finished. His words especially wrought in them a guilty consternation: 'They provoked Him to jealousy with strange gods, with abominations provoked they Him to anger. They sacrificed unto devils, not to God; to gods whom they knew not, to new gods that came newly up, whom your fathers feared not. Of the Rock that begat thee thou art unmindful, and hast forgotten God that formed thee. And when the LORD saw it, he abhorred them. They have moved me to jealousy with that which is not God.'

Some gnashed their teeth, others cried blasphemies, still others raised their maddened fists. Who was the Chronicler when compared to the people's gods.

But for Thiery, the Chronicler's words, heard in the voices of his enemies, were a comfort to his soul and an exhortation to earnestly contend for the faith; an exhortation which his young heart opened its doors to, and where, he wrote it upon the table therein.

The high-counselor nodded his head towards Squilby. Squilby grinned wickedly and departed.

As of yet, the crowd had nothing to vent its rage upon, for the Chronicler was not present. The high-counselor waited for them to quiet, and then he guided their attention to Staffsmitten — still standing before the judgment seat, alongside Diego Dandolo.

"And you Staffsmitten, do I understand correctly, that you also follow this God of Noah?"

Begging The Question

"Yes, Your Honor," Staffsmitten said. "I hope that it is most faithfully."

"Mawkish sentiments will only fuel the wrath of these people," drawled the high-counselor. "If you wish to curb their anger I would advise you to give us less of it; answer questions in a straightforward manner.

"Are you in agreement with the Chronicler, concerning your God of Noah — as far as you have heard in the testimonies given this morning?"

"Yes, Your Honor."

Again the people jumped to their feet with deafening shouts. Staffsmitten stood calmly; whether he awaited another question or the attack of an angry mob, he seemed indifferent.

The high-counselor held up a scroll and handed it to Staffsmitten. The people quieted. "Do you recognize it?"

"I do, Your Honor, it is the Book of Job."

"It is your very own copy. We've taken it from a cave, which I understand to be a Tump Barrow's gate, and you its gate keeper." This revelation stirred the amphitheatre to an excited buzz, for little was known of the Dwarven Brotherhood's realm. "We have a mind to be lenient with you, Staffsmitten. The king likes you. He thinks highly of your skills." The high-counselor shook his head sadly. "But he does not like some of the passages you've written in this book.

"For instance, you've written much about the grave — twelve times to be exact; in particular this passage is most disturbing to the king … let's see, I'll read a portion of it: *'As the cloud is consumed and vanisheth away: so he that goeth down to the grave shall come up no more. He shall return no more to his house, neither shall his place know him anymore.'*

"Worse yet, you mention hell twice. Hell must be removed from your story.

"You know the history of our kingdom, of King Frothgar and his search for the queen. Now that Strongbow has raised men to life, he wants his mother found and raised also … she died when he was yet very young. This passage you've written troubles him so that he does not sleep well. I know it will be a simple thing for you to change it and any other copies you know of, thereby keeping in the king's good graces. What have you to say, Staffsmitten?"

"I have much to say," Staffsmitten replied, standing tall and speaking with more authority than any council or king — Thiery noticed that he did not use the appellation, 'Your Honor'. "You have made three terrible mistakes. The Book of Job is not my story. I did not write it, but only copied the words from yet another copy. It is God's Word, it is the true telling of a man named Job, in a land called Uz, and God's dealings with him.

"If you removed the word 'sun' from that scroll, it would not make the sun disappear. No more can you make 'hell' or the 'grave' disappear by removing those words. And if you had read further you would see that there will be a raising of the dead to life. It reads: '*For I know that my redeemer liveth, and that he shall stand at the latter day upon the earth: And though after my skin worms destroy this body, yet in my flesh shall I see God* …'

"You see, there will be a resurrection of the dead one day. God Himself will stand upon the earth. The dead, small and great, will stand before God. The sea will give up the dead in it; and death and hell will deliver up the dead which are in them, and death and hell will be cast into the lake of fire."

The high-counselor and his judges shrank back before Staffsmitten. The whole assembly sat frozen, quiet, and wide-eyed.

Staffsmitten continued, "Your final mistake was to think that I would dare change the Word of God. Add thou not unto his words, lest He reprove thee, and thou be found a liar. If any man shall add unto these things, God shall add unto him the plagues that are written in this book: And if any man shall take away from the words —"

"Enough!" the high-counselor was angry. "Even if God had sent these words to men, surely they have been corrupted by other men before now. What is to stop us from changing them ourselves?"

"God."

"Come now," the high-counselor laughed. "Do you mean to tell me, that if I were to try and make a copy of this scroll, yet change some words, that your God would stop me?"

"You can try to change that copy if you like," Staffsmitten said, "and you may even succeed, but you cannot change the Book of Job for God has protected it so that it will endure to all generations, every word of it. Even if that were the original, God will preserve His Word."

The high-counselor chuckled derisively. "Do you think me a fool?"

Staffsmitten paused, "The grass withereth, the flower fadeth: but the word of our God shall stand for ever! The scripture cannot be broken! The words of the Lord are pure words: as silver tried in a furnace of earth, purified seven times …" Then Staffsmitten gazed heavenward, a look of such joy upon his face. "… Thou shalt keep them, O Lord, thou shalt preserve them from this generation for ever."

"Pure? Do you mean to say that there are no errors in the Book of Job?" The high-counselor's eyes narrowed, he rubbed his fingers against one another.

"There are none, Your Honor."

"Would you stake your life on it?"

"I would, Your Honor."

"Answer me then. Your book has God asking Job if he has entered into the springs of the sea? All of our learned men say there is no such thing. Have you proof of them? Have you seen these springs of the sea? And this ridiculous statement that says the earth hangs on nothing — it is your life which hangs, and by a thread about to be cut."

"I have not seen the springs in the sea or how the earth hangs on nothing, but you will find it impossible to prove it is an error, Your Honor."

"What do you mean? It is obvious. Judges, what do you say?"

"Error! Wrong-minded! Foolishness! He rants!" The judges smiled at themselves.

"Your Honor, esteemed judges, have you ever seen the earth hanging on anything? Have you proof that it hangs on something? Have you scoured the depths of the seas? Have you been in every place upon its bottom? If not, then you have no proof that these are errors.

"You have simply assumed what you are trying to prove. You say the Book of Job has errors in it, and by what proof? None have been given. Do you, Your Honor, have a reason beyond arbitrary assumptions that this book is indeed in error?"

Staffsmitten continued, "I know what God has said and I believe Him. I hope you shall believe Him too, one day."

The judges looked to the high-counselor for a refutation.

None was forthcoming. The high-counselor reddened and then became wholly inflamed. "Our proof comes from our learned men. They say that these are errors. It is enough!"

"Your Honor, I would like to point out that the Chronicler and myself are learned men, yet we do not concur with yours. And anyway, an appeal to authority hardly proves your point.

"Give me a boy from this crowd, who has heard your arguments and mine, and let us hear what he shall say. For even a child can see the logical shortcomings put forth."

"A child indeed!" The high-counselor snarled rabidly. But then he seemed to notice the crowd's favorable animation upon hearing this request, and then he looked into the dark tunnel, nestled into the amphitheatre's heart. Thiery turned in time to see some flickering movement.

The high-counselor grimaced, but only for a second; now his face was a mask. "Yes then… a boy." The mask was slipping. He struggled to control himself. "You've heard the request. Is there any boy who would stand before this council and give an opinion to the logic of these proceedings?"

It was an amazing request for Staffsmitten to make; for who would dare point out the logical shortcomings of the high-counselor. There was a sense of fair play amongst the people, but it was easily quenched by appeals to their false gods versus the one true God — all fairness instantly dissipated when their gods were condemned.

Any boy coming forward might even be beaten.

While Thiery had never met Staffsmitten, he had stayed in his home, eaten his food, read his books, and learned of his love for God. Thiery had greatly admired him. But now, to Thiery, Staffsmitten was a hero, a true keeper of the Word — nobly standing for truth against frightful opposition.

Thiery stood up.

Pip tried to pull him back.

Clum, the guard, also reached a hand towards him. But Thiery was already moving forward to stand alongside Staffsmitten and Diego Dandolo.

Posthumous Execution

Staffsmitten smiled warmly at Thiery. Diego looked at him and furrowed his brow, as if he were trying to recall something.

"I will give my opinion, sir," Thiery said, and then suddenly realizing his mistake, added, "Your Honor."

The red blotches multiplied upon the high-counselor's face and neck. "How old are you?"

"Thirteen, Your Honor, just a little big for my age." This last, Thiery added, when he was met with a disbelieving look.

The high-counselor glanced toward the dark tunnel again. "Yes then, young enough. And your name?"

"My name's Thiery, Your Honor."

Diego Dandolo's head turned quickly towards him.

"Thiery, son of whom?" the high-counselor asked.

"I do not know, Your Honor, but I was raised by Oded the Bear. He's my guardian."

This caused another wave of excited chatter to roll across the amphitheater; Oded the Bear was a hero to all of Hradcanny.

"Do not make up stories, boy, or the council will treat you badly."

"It's true, Your Honor. If you know where he is, you can ask him."

"Do I understand then that you do not know where he is?"

"I don't, Your Honor, but I'd very much like to know."

"How did you come to lose your guardian?"

"The Dragon Priests and my father, they sacrificed me."

The crowd gasped. The high-counselor leaned forward as much as his girth would allow. "I thought you did not know who your father was, and are you trying to say that you also have been brought back to life? Foolish boy. I've caught you easily enough, we shall see how long you stick to your lies. Take the whip to him. Guard!"

Thiery held the high-counselor's stare with a confidence born of truth. "You may strike me if you like, Your Honor, but I have not lied to you. The sacrifice did not work because I dropped the poisoned food on the ground and was only able to eat a bit of it. Then I heard, but did not see, a man speaking to Count Rosencross, just outside my tent. That man claimed to be my father, and thinking I was dead, spoke of his sacrificing me to the Dragon. The Count did not seem to be pleased—"

"I mean no disrespect, Your Honor," Staffsmitten interrupted, "but I thought you asked this boy here to give us an answer concerning the logic of our arguments. Instead, you bully him concerning his parentage, and threaten to have him whipped. I withdraw my request therefore, and ask that the boy be allowed to return to his seat."

"No disrespect indeed! I have called a witness, and we shall hear his testimony. You mock me with your insolence; you followers of Noah's God shall be put in your place. The king no longer smiles upon your kind, the gods hate you, and the followers of those gods have hearts that grow cold against you.

"High and mighty you are, but low and miserable you shall become. Tell me, Staffsmitten, how many of your kind do you think sit within this amphitheatre now?"

"I could not know, Your Honor, I hope that there are many."

The high-counselor lifted his arm and pointed his finger at the crowds; slowly he dragged that fearful appendage across the amphitheatre, pointing, pointing, glaring … then his words echoed against the public's silent stare: "You see where it leads, this following of the God of Noah … the gods will not allow it much longer … the king no longer smiles upon them … the people will rise up against them … the council will crush them." Then he smiled wickedly and raised his voice. "Come forward, all here who claim to follow the 'one true God of Noah'!"

No one stirred. A few averted their eyes.

The high-counselor laughed. "You are very much alone, Staffsmitten and Diego Dandolo, very much alone."

"It gladdens my heart," Staffsmitten replied, "to have such an opportunity to speak of God to you and the people seated before us. I am afraid for you, Your Honor, and for the secret counsel of the wicked; who whet their tongue like a sword, and bend their bows to shoot their arrows, even bitter words:

"That they may shoot in secret at the perfect: suddenly do they shoot at him, and fear not. They encourage themselves in an evil matter: they commune of laying snares privily; they say, Who shall see them?

"But God shall shoot at them with an arrow; suddenly shall they be wounded. So they shall make their own tongue to fall upon themselves: all that see them shall flee away, and evil shall hunt the violent man to overthrow him. I am afraid for you, Your Honor, for I can see that the evil hunter shall one day find you. I pray you will repent."

Sweat broke out upon the high-counselor's brow. He shook, with fear or rage, or both, it was hard to tell. But he had not found his voice yet, and so Staffsmitten continued.

"Yes, it gladdens my heart, Your Honor, to testify of God before you who follow other gods. But it pains me greatly," here Staffsmitten looked imploringly at the crowd, "that the saints of God are not here to be encouraged by this, my defense."

Still no one made any movement to show that they too were a follower of Noah's God. Surely, there must be some within the amphitheatre — was the fear of man so great upon their hearts that they did nothing?

As Thiery listened, he did not fully grasp the import of what he was hearing, and how it was further instilling within him a steadfast resolution to follow the God of Noah wherever that might lead and whatever the consequences.

In a very real way, God was Father to the fatherless. Additionally, Thiery was fortunate to have men in his life, heroic men, like Lord McDougal, Oded, Staffsmitten, and even Gimcrack — men of God. Within Thiery's bones, the fire burned to which he could not sit still, nor stay his mouth.

"I am here, a saint of God," Thiery answered, "and I am encouraged."

Whatever force held back the high-counselor's tongue, it was now unleashed. "You vile, boy! You young villain and traitor, where and of whom did you learn to call yourself a saint of God?"

"From Oded the bear, Your Honor, and from those saints he brought me in contact with — those who taught me truth. Even more though, my faith in God, was established by reading the Book of Job."

At this, the high-counselor almost screamed in agony. "Do you see, my judges, what this poisonous book has done?"

"Poison!" The judges screamed; they looked like rabid animals. "It poisons those who read it! Curses upon

Staffsmitten! He's poisoned a boy's mind! Who knows how many more he's infected!"

"This foundling boy has no rights," the high-counselor said, seeming to gain control of himself at the sight of his judges, who had worked themselves into a state of froth and spittle; perhaps he realized that he too was mirroring that image and found it unflattering. "But we will be merciful upon his soul. Bring forth the whip, we shall soon change his mind."

"No, Your Honor," Diego Dandolo raised his voice. "He is not a foundling boy that you can whip upon the council's whim. An ætheling stands before you, and as you know, a young noble cannot be treated with so lowly a punishment."

"Ætheling?" the high-counselor's face turned pale, yet he was suspicious. "What proof have we? The boy said himself that he did not know his father's name."

"He does not, Your Honor, but the Chronicler does. How do you think someone like Oded the Bear came to be his guardian; the Chronicler himself appointed him."

"Tell us then, whose son is he?"

"I cannot. You must ask the Chronicler if you wish to know."

Thiery's head spun — the Chronicler! *Oded was appointed by the Chronicler; and he knows my father. And my father is a noble, and I, a noble youth, an ætheling?*

"We will take a moment to discuss these things." The high-counselor waved his judges closer. "You shall have our verdict forthwith."

The judges and high-counselor were soon interrupted by a messenger — one who came from the tunnel, where the darkness hid some secret spectator. Thiery thought it likely to be the king himself, or a trusted advisor to the king. For Clum had said it was rumored he was here, and the high-counselor constantly brought his gaze to rest upon the tunnel's mouth. He opened the messenger's missive with eager, shaking hands.

The high-counselor finished the letter, spoke a few hushed words to the judges, and then cleared his throat. "Staffsmitten, by the laws of the land and the king, this high council of Hradcanny finds you guilty of blasphemy against the gods. The sentence is posthumous execution by stoning, after which your body shall be thrown over the northern wall into the dumping grounds. You are not to be buried; you will be left to the beasts. Judges?"

"Death by stoning!"

"Death!"

"Over the northern wall!"

"Food for the beasts!"

The crowd mumbled their approval. Staffsmitten turned to young Thiery, and spoke quickly, "I'm proud of you ætheling. You've strengthened me for my final trial. Though, in truth, I look forward to it, to see our King of Kings, to hear Him say well done, good and faithful servant.

"You have stood this day as a witness to your God and to His Word. Remember, do not forget — God and His Word are inseparable. His Word shall be preserved and you, aetheling, may even be one of those He uses to accomplish it upon this earth — the preservation of His perfect Word. Remember that we are His loresmen. Until we meet again young saint — for this God is our God forever and ever: He will be our guide even unto death."

The guards took Staffsmitten away; Clum was one of them. A large contingent of the crowd followed, picking up stones from the stoning mound as they left the amphitheatre.

"Ætheling Thiery," the high-counselor was doing his best to sound respectful. "The king wishes for you to attend the heroes' banquet tomorrow night at dusk. Your guardian, Oded the Bear, will be attending. Do not keep the king or his guests waiting. You will come, yes?"

"Thank you, Your Honor, I will."

The high-counselor handed Thiery a cold coin. "Compliments of the king — you must come better dressed. Will you need assistance?"

Thiery did not know if he would or not, but thankfully Diego Dandolo stepped forward. "If the young lord will have me, Your Honor, I shall assist him."

Thiery nodded his head. "Thank you, sir."

The high-counselor eyed Diego with wariness and maybe something more too. "Very well then." He waved his hand through the air and turned his eager attention upon the merchants; they bowed with groveling smiles and raised steaming plates of food.

None of the guards were eager to touch him now that it was over; the rocks had all been thrown and the crowd's anger appeased; they slunk away, ashamed at the blood on their hands. Clum bent over the lifeless body and lifted Staffsmitten into his arms. Clum was a powerfully built man and needed no help from the others. They offered none.

"Your goin' the wrong way, Clum." One of the guards said.

"No, I'm not."

"The council said we had to throw him over the northern wall."

"Aye, they did."

"You're goin' the wrong way then."

"He was a friend," Clum explained. "I'll still put him where he's supposed to end up, but I can't throw a friend over the wall like that. I aim to lay him down gently."

The other guards looked at each other. Then they shrugged and followed Clum to the northern gate. From there it was only a short distance to the dumping grounds. It smelled terrible and they were anxious to get away.

Clum set Staffsmitten down, leaned him against a tree near the woods, and put a scroll in his lap.

"Is that the book he got himself killed for?" another guard asked.

Clum frowned. "It is. He set special store by it. Can't say I understand why, but I've seen enough battles to know a brave man when I see one. When my time comes, I hope I'm half the man that he was."

Clum and the guards walked away in silence.

Darts

The Chronicler sat at his desk. He spent a lot of time sitting there of late, composing words of intrigue rather than histories or godly exhortations. He could sense a change in the king and his counselors, and in the way Master Squilby acted. Some of the newly hired servants of the Citadel did not always act servant-like, as if that wasn't their real duty. The sneaks were certainly turning up at every corner.

So, the Chronicler did not retire, as he thought he would, at the end of the games. Instead, he decided it was simply time to go, to disappear, and many would he bring with him. By keeping his position as Master of the Citadel it gave him a better vantage from which to make things happen. But it must be a secret or the king might try to stop them.

Everything was in place. The last pigeon parchments set before him, ready to be paired with their carriers; they were the final orders, and once sent, there would be no turning back. Soon he would feel the roll of his ship underfoot.

But the children must be found first. He was anxious to meet them. The Chronicler thought back over the years to the many reports of young Thiery's love of God and his boldness. He thought of Tostig's note describing the events leading up to his rescue from Igi Forkbeard and how Thiery had bravely proclaimed the truths of God.

The Chronicler smiled and spoke to the empty room, "At least I have fulfilled my commission in that, Johanna. You would have been pleased; your son has so clear the light of God upon him, that he blinds the wicked with it, and shines upon their darkness. Though yet a boy, he is truly a man of God, one which God might use to make up the hedge and stand in the gap."

There was a sound; something out of place in the chamber beyond.

"I've heard you Diego," The Chronicler said, without looking up from his work. "You'll not sneak up on me today. But do come in, we have some things to discuss."

The Chronicler began folding his parchments.

With his eyes on his work, a part of him noted the door opening. Again, something was out of place.

Still not looking up, he gave a little more of his attention to the door as it opened. That was it. The door had given its initial reluctant creek as it always did when first unlatched, but where were the familiar sounds that should have followed, if it had continued to open?

Diego Dandolo would not peek in upon his master, nor would anyone else for that matter … unless.

The Chronicler reached for a large leather bound tome on the corner of his desk as he glanced at the door. The door was indeed open a crack. A bulging eye looked at him.

He knew that eye.

A thin tube, grasped by Squilby's grimy fingers, was aimed in the Chronicler's direction — a blow-dart — and there could be little doubt that it was poisoned. Squilby had waited before shooting it, the Chronicler thought, because he wanted the Chronicler to know who it was that had killed him.

The dart was almost impossible to see, just a blurring of the air as it came at him. He raised the leather tome just in time. He heard the thud of the dart. Yet he felt the tiniest pain in his hand. No, it was fast becoming a firebrand.

The dart held his little finger pegged to the tome. Squilby pulled the door closed; footsteps grew faint as he made his way into the hall.

There were several poisons of which Squilby had access. The Citadel's apothecaries knew of many and had developed more. The Yew tree had a gloomy, and terrifying appearance; terrifying because of its berries which contained a strong alkaloid poison — one that brought sudden death through the heart.

Or possibly it was Belladonna, the deadly Nightshade flower; first there would be dizziness, then raving agitation, then coma, and then death; no, it was not likely Belladonna, that would be too slow.

Perhaps Hemlock. It would congeal and chill the blood, or Wolfsbane which first acts as a stimulant and then paralyzes the nervous system, the limbs go numb, and then death. Always death.

It could be snake venom or, even more potent than a cobra, the blister beetle, containing one of the most dangerous animal toxins known to man.

These thoughts were just a flitting impression that flashed through his mind; the Chronicler knew his time was very short … Squilby would make sure that he had seconds only, unless …

He unsheathed his dagger, drew it back, and struck.

Better to lose a finger and live … well, maybe not live, but it would buy him some time. He ran to the fire, and seared the stump. Already his body was acting strange, the poison was spreading.

He would have to work quickly.

Thiery had grown up in an age when men lost their lives often; to the whims of kings and chieftains, from battles and arguments settled in violence, from sickness, from sacrifices, from serpents, dragons and wolves, from brigands and pirates, and more. And the telling of the tales of death were more common even than the death itself, so that a boy became habituated to its insistent presence.

But every time a man took his last breath, Thiery wondered at it. He thought about the person's soul. Where would they live out eternity? More often than not, Thiery mourned for them.

Thiery did not mourn for Staffsmitten; he was a man who knew where he was going, and he knew that God looked forward to their meeting, that God even loved the death of his saints. Thiery thought that knowing such a thing must give one peace and courage to meet death bravely; he hoped that he too would be ready when his time came.

They walked in silence, Diego Dandolo, Pip, and Thiery.

The meeting with Oded at tomorrow's dinner popped into his mind, and then Suzie's face … what a blessing for his little sister, to feel the safety of Oded again. She talked about him often, and Lord McDougal, he would probably be there also… and the king himself would be at the dinner, what would that be like? … Yet that would all happen tomorrow. What about this very day? He was about to meet the great Chronicler. Would he tell him who his mother and father were? According to Diego Dandolo they were nobles. But why had it been kept a secret from him? It seemed that there were forces at work to keep him alive and there were forces, like his own father, desiring his death. His mind raced back to the king's dinner … would there be Dragon Priests there?

Diego stopped abruptly; he stiffened, his eyes scanning the crowds, shops and alleys. Pip too, was on edge.

"This way." Diego turned on the next street, but it was in the wrong direction if they were going to the Citadel. They moved quickly through the crowds, then Diego, alerted to something, would turn their small party still further and further from the Citadel and from the Chronicler.

"I'm a fool!" Diego Dandolo snarled. He did not seem like a man to become easily agitated. Thiery could not see an enemy, but he could sense danger prickling along his spine.

They halted in a bright square, near a horse and carriage. "They're steering us further away from the Citadel."

"If you please, sir?" Pip's voice was urgent.

"Go on."

"I've spotted five sneaks so far as I'm sure you have, sir. But we're also bein' steered towards an open window up there; I caught a glimpse of a Death-Hound Rider in it. It was Austri Half-Cat, I'd know him anywhere, and he had a dart gun. I'm thinkin' a few more feet and you'll have a dart in you, sir."

"Run back the way we came, just like you've been trained, only don't go so fast as to lose Thiery. I'll rendezvous with you at the amphitheatre, we'll use its tunnel to get underground; by now it should be empty. From there it's a short distance to the Citadel. We'll split up so as to weaken their numbers and maybe confuse —"

A dagger with glistening tip shot out from under the carriage they'd been standing next to. Diego's leg had been there just seconds before. Thiery didn't know how he had moved out of the way so fast, and in the same instant, Diego's own blade was in his hand flashing. "Run boys, run!"

It was all Thiery could do to keep up with Pip as he dodged in and out of people, animals, and streets.

He wondered if a glistening dart or dagger would come for them too.

He prayed.

Death Of An Elder

The Chronicler was sitting on the floor, just below the window, when Diego Dandolo and the two boys entered the chamber. His back was to the wall, his head slumped forward, and the window was open.

Diego closed the door and locked it. "Stay away from that window. Pip, gather all the papers on his desk and whatever you find within."

Crawling to the Chronicler's side, Diego's face was grim. He reached slowly out and touched the limp wrist. Diego sighed. "We didn't plan for this, sir. How could we possibly know that they would come for you. The king must have gone mad then, and they've poisoned his mind against you.

"I'd like to thank you, sir, for taking me in, for telling me of your God … and I'll do my best for the children. I've found Thiery … I brought him to see you, and you were right about him, he's a fine lad."

He looked down at the angry-red stump where the Chronicler's finger had been, then at a dart in his neck. Diego turned to Thiery. "Keep down and don't move from this spot, I'll be right back." He rolled over to a hanging tapestry near the fire place and disappeared behind it. In a moment he reappeared, ran to the desk, and then crawled back to the Chronicler's side.

He addressed him once again, though by now, it was clear to Thiery that the Chronicler no longer lived. "They got you at your desk, sir, but you out figured them with your quick thinking. Yet they got you again when you came to the window. But, I see you've sent all the pigeons on errands; I imagine you've set things to rolling. But what instructions do you have for me, I wonder?

"I look forward to seeing you again soon, sir. Perhaps it will be very soon."

As if to emphasize these last words, someone pushed against the chamber's door, only to find it locked. They pushed harder. There were whispered words.

Pip crawled over, eyes wide. "If you please, sir," he whispered, "I've put everything in this sack, all but this. I don't know, but it had some blood on it, and so I thought maybe he wrote it most recent-like, and it had your initials at the top."

Diego Dandolo spread the parchment between his fingers:

DD
Travel by mountains hall,
to see not the daughter of the not giant lord,
not out of the yellow and blues marriage,
bow-bender

"Well done, Pip. That's where I'll find my instructions."

Pip smiled with face stretching pleasure. No doubt, he did not hear those words often, not when Squilby was his master.

"Okay boys, follow me. Quiet as a mouse."

Diego slipped behind the tapestry. The ceiling was low and the passage was narrow and gloomy. It smelled, and then Thiery saw why. As they followed it to the end it opened into a large stone walled pigeon coup. There were slits on either side with fresh air passing through, but not wide enough for a bird; and there was light streaming down from a turret of windows above.

"We'll climb up there, the window on the far left is unlocked, and greased. It's positioned so that anyone watching the coup from below won't see us exit onto the roof. We'll wait up there till dusk just to be sure no one see's us. Now put these on, soot your faces and hands a bit, and then up with you. You're chimney sweeps now, boys."

When dusk finally came, Thiery thought that once again he'd likely not be where he was supposed to be. He wondered how Suzie and Percival were getting along. Lord McDougal never came back for her, then Gimcrack disappeared, and now Thiery and Pip would be hard pressed to make it back tonight. He didn't mean to sigh so loud, but it was too late to recall. Pip and Diego glanced at him.

"Sorry, I was just thinking of Suzie, and hoping she wasn't scared."

"Scared!" Pip looked affronted. "Why Percival is with her, how can she be scared?"

Thiery smiled. It was infectious, the complete trust Pip had in his little brother. "You're right, Pip, what a great blessing that Percival is there to protect her."

Pip's honor was assuaged. "Yes, he's the best." Then Pip looked at Diego. "Sir, if you don't want to tell me, I do understand, but that parchment is makin' my head hurt. Do you know what it means?"

Diego smiled. "It's a game the Chronicler and I play … " He stopped short, then continued, "… used to play. Using an unusual poetic play on words we would give each other messages." He raised his eyebrow slightly, "In case they were to fall into the hands of a sneak, like you."

"Oh. Oh, I see."

"If you were no longer a sneak, but instead you were to be my student — understand, that I am no longer part of the Citadel, and I do not know where events will take us, but if you will be my student and assistant, then perhaps I could explain.

"Before you answer though, understand this. Thiery is an ætheling, and the Chronicler planned first to protect him and then to promote him. Thiery will be your and my lord if you choose to throw in with me. Is that understood young, Pip."

Pip looked at Thiery and Diego with something like awe and pride. "I would be most honored to be both your servants." Pip smiled, embarrassed. "Did I say that right enough?"

"As well as the highest king's counselor, Pip. Well said." Diego smiled warmly. "Now, it is almost dusk, so we shall spend the last minutes, unless we are discovered sooner, examining the Chronicler's note. It is simple really. *Travel by mountain's hall.* Tell me Thiery, what is a chieftain's hall?"

"His home, where he lives."

"Yes, and where do mountains live? What is their home? Where do they dwell?"

"In the sky?"

"Quite right. So we are to travel by sky. What can that mean? Perhaps it will become clearer as we decipher the rest. We are traveling to see someone who is not a daughter … hmm … then what?"

Pip jumped in. "A son?"

"You boys are impressive."

Pip couldn't keep back the giggle behind his smile.

"I think I know the next part, sir," Thiery offered. "A not giant lord then would be a dwarf lord?"

"Precisely. We must travel by sky to meet the son of the dwarf lord. You'll not know who that is though, I'm sure."

"That would be Cnutfoot." Thiery said.

Diego stared at Thiery, something like surprise, maybe even admiration in his eyes. Now Thiery was embarrassed.

Diego resumed his questioning, "Okay then, what does the rest mean? 'Not out of the yellow's and blue's marriage, bow-bender."

"I think I've already got it, but I must admit that it makes no sense to me." Thiery said.

"Please proceed."

"Not out must mean in. Yellow and blue if they were to unite in marriage, become one flesh as it were, then they would be green. And a bow-bender may be an archer. But I don't understand its meaning."

Pip's mouth suddenly dropped open. "The Inn of the Green Archer!" he whispered the words as if he were about to meet the greatest hero on earth.

The Green Archer

Three chimney sweeps traveled Hradcanny's sky-road: the rooftop's of the city. It was a common enough place to catch a glimpse of slender black-sooted forms, carrying their brush, and disappearing into the dark towering smokestacks known as chimneys.

Those vertical brick tunnels were dark enough inside, and no chimney-sweep in his right mind worked his trade in the evening, for the light of the sun, coming through the chimney-top was meagerly and precious. But the men of the chimneys were also men of the rooftop sky-road; for that is what is was to them; a place of escape from the city's tumult and smells; and when they crawled out of the most dark and confining places a man could find work in — excepting maybe the sewers — the chimney-sweeps had a world to themselves with clean air, and space about them, and beautiful views. They were proud of their rooftop sky-road, and protective of it, wary that somehow the city below would discover its grandeur and come pouring up over the building's edges to spoil their sanctuary.

A large block of red bricks rose up before them; six chimney-flues, each as wide as a man, poked from its summit. Smoke came out of three, two were empty black holes, and one was capped. Another building, slightly taller, placed the whole structure in shadow.

"When you come to the wooden rung," Diego whispered, "reach behind you, you'll find a passage. That's our way in."

Diego Dandolo climbed nimbly up, lifted the cap off the chimney, and motioned the boys to climb in. Pip went first, then Thiery. Diego followed, replacing the cap, closing off even the moon's meager light. Thiery thought it well that Gimcrack did not have to join them for Diego did not even strike a light; he smiled, suddenly missing his friend.

It was obvious that this chimney had not been used in a long time, if ever. There was no soot or creosote, and it would have made little sense to have a wooden rung upon the ladder somewhere below.

It seemed that they descended for a long time, metal rung after metal rung, and still they clambered down. He sensed that Pip was not below him any longer, the air changed slightly, and then his hand felt wood, less smooth than the metal, and less cold to the touch. But if he hadn't been looking for it, he'd never have paid it any attention.

It was a short step into the dark beyond. It was still a tight passage, but larger by far than the chimney they left behind. It was exciting to be part of all these secret places and tunnels, even while Thiery knew that such things existed because of dangerous men and dangerous times, he couldn't help but feel the thrill of it. He knew Pip felt the same. Just then Diego lit a lamp, and Pip's lithe body was poised in its high-strung way. There was no fear in his eyes, just wild gleeful enthusiasm.

Pip risked a whisper, "Thank you, sir, thank you." He looked at Diego Dandolo with such adoration that Thiery's heart also welled within him; he felt moved to the same feelings of love and fierce loyalty that Pip's countenance was expressing better than any words could.

He was an æthleing now, a youngling lord, and already he had two retainers. They would do all for him, he knew; and he must do all for them.

If Pip grew into a man anything like Diego Dandolo, and he could see it would likely be so, then Thiery would be a very blessed lord indeed. For he had observed Diego closely from the time of Staffsmitten's trial until now, less than a day for sure, but in that time he'd witnessed a man who stood boldly for God and for his fellow saint even when the world boiled around him in enmity. Diego didn't hesitate to persevere in his duty, and those duties had been wisely done.

And he was fast, like no other person Thiery had seen, every step, every movement of his head spoke of a capable and dangerous warrior, though slight of stature; this too could be an asset, for men would misjudge his capabilities.

They hurried along passages, some lined with cut stone, and some cut through stone, until they reached a non-descript bend in the path.

"Before now, only the Chronicler and myself knew of this door. I will share it with you. Everything I will show you now must be kept a secret." Diego Dandolo did not wait for an answer. He slid a rock which was very near the ground, there was the slight sound of a bolt scraping, then he pushed low and part of the wall, pivoting at its center, swung half of its length into the passage, and half its length into the chamber beyond.

Crawling through, the boys followed. He closed the secret door, and slid a similar rock upon the other side, again they heard the scraping of a bolt.

The room was in a state of disarray, as if someone were moving in, or perhaps moving out.

"Forgive me, boys." Diego actually looked self-conscious. "I've already transferred most of my things to the ship, and it was done rather hastily. I so hate to have a mess about me. Let us at least clean ourselves up, then I shall have a look at the Chronicler's papers, and then we shall go into the Inn."

There were two doors leading out of Diego's room. Behind one they could hear the sounds of talk, laughter, the clinking of dinner-ware — they hadn't eaten since that morning, and it was well after dark now. Thiery looked longingly at that door.

"Pip," Diego spoke as he removed his chimney-sweep garb, "who do you, and the sneaks, think the Green Archer is?"

"You, sir! Well … sort of. If Master Squilby wasn't always sayin' so, we'd not think it. For often, after some grand thing the Green Archer does, our investigatin' it or even some of the sneaks tell us hows it couldn't of been you, cause you were seen to have been somewheres else. Are you about to tell us who it is?"

"I am."

Pip's eyes were as wide as his gaping mouth. "You mean … 'I am', as in you're gonna tell us, or 'I am', as in you are the Green Archer?"

"Both." Diego turned away, but not until Thiery saw the beginnings of a grin.

Pip couldn't speak.

When Diego looked back all traces of his smile were gone. "But remember, Pip, this is not a game, men's lives are at stake."

"Oh," Pip gasped, his head nodding vigorously, "I know, yes, sir, I do." He still stared at Diego Dandolo in awe. "But, sir, how'd ya do it? I mean, we've seen you in two places at the same time."

"No, Pip, the sneaks thought they saw me in two places at the same time for we both know that is impossible."

"Yes, sir, quite right." Pip plodded on, "But, I don't understand."

"Have you heard of the Thespian Society, the actor's guild?"

Pip nodded his head.

"Do you know who Gettlefinger is?"

Pip laughed, "Everyone knows who he is. I told Percival I'd take him to see one of his shows some day. Percival's mighty excited to see a real play, so I figured I'd take him to see the best."

"Yes, well, Gettlefinger has played the part of Diego Dandolo, while I have played the part of the Green Archer, though I think he plays me rather stiffly. Anyway, he and I share a close resemblance to begin with, and he is a master of disguise, and more importantly he is a loyal friend."

Diego paused and looked from Pip to Thiery, a deep penetrating stare. "By telling you who the Green Archer is and of Gettlefinger's role, I am teaching you, I am giving you understanding … but I have put a man's life at risk by doing so. Do you understand?"

The boys nodded their heads solemnly.

"Good. Give instruction to a wise man, and he will be yet wiser: teach a just man, and he will increase in learning. But never forget that there is but one path by which you can truly be a wise and just man — the fear of the LORD is the beginning of wisdom: and the knowledge of the holy is understanding.

"Thiery. We have a difficulty to contend with. Circumstances demand that we move quickly. Young Pip and I have pledged ourselves to you as our lord. I have taken the reigns from you, I have made every decision, and I have not even asked your counsel. My counsel now is that I continue in this role while this current crisis persists; I already know much of the Chronicler's plans, I know the city, and I know our enemies. Of course, you may at any time, reverse our roles as you see fit. What do you think of the arrangement?" Diego Dandolo raised his eyebrows expectantly.

Thiery felt a surge of relief. For being an ætheling would take some getting used to, but actually having command over men, while he was just a boy, seemed terrifying.

"I would like it very much, sir. And I think that we should not let others know what I am, as far as possible. Anyway, I don't even know much about myself, do I?"

"I think," Diego began as he drew out a small bundle of papers from his breast, "that something in here shall tell you more. I retrieved these from a hidden compartment in the Chronicler's desk. At least some of it concerns you, I'm sure." He hesitated slightly while pulling at his mustache. "Shall we open it?"

There was an eagerness in Diego Dandolo's face that Thiery thought must be reflected in his own. "I would like that, sir, I would like it very much."

Diego's hands trembled as he unwrapped the bundle. There were four packets. The first was protected by two wax seals. Scribbled on the front were the words: *'Chronicler's Will. It is my desire that this be opened upon my ship in the presence of three witnesses.'*

Diego shrugged his shoulders slightly, "I hope the other two will allay at least some of our curiosity."

The rest were not sealed. The second was a map showing much of the known world, though there were many empty spaces; and the third was a map detailing the region in and around Hradcanny. Thiery pointed at the dotted lines upon the land. "What do these represent, sir?"

Diego pointed at the large island country where Bannockburn Castle lay, across the sea from Hradcanny. "The Chronicler thought that after another fifty or hundred years there might not be a sea between Bannockburn and Hradcanny. The warm waters of the oceans, meeting with the cold air of the continents have accumulated massive mountains of ice inland, especially as you travel further north, and as they continue to grow, the ocean waters recede.

"Hard to imagine I know, but if the trend reverses some day, and the Chronicler thinks it shall — then woe to the men who build cities too low. That dotted line is the Chronicler's best guess as to where the waters might rise."

Thiery was gripped with a sudden flash of understanding. "Hradcanny and Bannockburn, and many others would all be under the sea then!"

"Yes." Diego's face was grim. "But in any event, if it does happen, it should not be for hundreds of years. Ah, now, look here, this last packet is a letter that the Chronicler has never let me see; he has only hinted at its contents. But I know they involve you, young Thiery."

He handed the letter to Thiery. But was there something in Diego Dandolo's manner? A slight difficulty in swallowing? A fire in the eyes? Thiery guessed that it was not without a struggle that Diego gave up the letter.

Thiery placed it back in Deigo's hands. "We must hurry. Perhaps you could read it aloud. You will no doubt, know better what to make of it, sir."

Diego bowed his head slightly, "Thank you, Thiery, it is good of you."

He cleared his throat and began: 'My dear Grandfather—"

They were interrupted by a pounding at the door.

A voice boomed from the other side, "Deigo Dandolo? Are you holed up in there? I've been waiting patiently all of ten minutes! We under-folk are always waiting upon the whims of others, but I did not think you would practice such unfriendly behavior."

Thiery recognized the musical baritone at once.

Diego folded the letter with painful reluctance and handed it to Thiery. "Hide it upon your person," he whispered, then more loudly he turned to the door, "It seems an uncouth and discourteous tongue wags at our door, forcing us to be hospitable or suffer the consequences!"

It almost sounded like a chuckle beyond, but Thiery couldn't be sure.

The voice of Cnutfoot answered, "Insults from cheeky underlings stab through this thick timber well enough, but remove the barricade you whimpering dolt, and meet the steel of my sword's thundering bolt."

Diego wrenched the door open.

Cnutfoot squeezed his wide bulk through the opening and grabbed Diego in a great bear hug. "It does me good to see you, Diego, and look who I've brought along."

All faces turned to see.

Cnutfoot bellowed the introduction, "'Tis none other than Gimcrack, maker of maps and witty inventions, and most notably, slayer of giants. Every too-tall oaf within a hundred leagues will have heard of Gimcrack the giant slayer, and they'll shudder in their boots."

Gimcrack gulped, his face reddened, his eye twitched, and he forced a toothy-lippy smile.

Mortimer

"I don't like it out here, Elvodug. We're just a sittin' here waitin' to be somethin's dinner." Flemup looked genuinely scared.

"Go add more wood to the fire you chicken-fritter, that'll keep stuff away." Elvodug didn't like it either, but he wasn't about to show Flemup how frightened he was.

"The only problem with that, you flathead," Flemup retorted angrily, "is that we'll run out of wood before the night's over, and whose goin' to get more out there in the dark? I'm tellin' you right now, it ain't gonna be me. I don't plan on gettin' eat up."

Elvodug couldn't hold back the ire rising in his belly. "You blunder-oaf, if you'd have climbed down that rope quicker, we wouldn't be in this predicament now. Would we? You just sat there and watched that little animal carry Suzie away."

"Little animal? That little animal was bigger than you and that flabby belly of yours, and there was at least five more of 'em near the woods. I'd a been a sittin' duck down there while you were safe and sound above."

"Now, Flemup," Elvodug protested irritably, "you know how my hands cramp. The plan was for you to shimmy down, and me to meet you around."

"That's where the whole fault lies, right there, right there!" Flemmup pointed his finger in Elvodug's face. "It was that dumb plan. Whose dumb plan? Your plan, your dumb plan! We aint never gonna track down that girl, and if we do, how we gonna get her away from them beasts? I tell you, somethin's gonna eat us!"

"Would you stop sayin' that!" Elvodug's face grew hot; he could feel Flemup's wild fevered words maddening him like one of them berserkers. "Somethin's gonna eat us! Somethin's gonna eat us! All you ever talk about is food. How am I gonna sleep if you keep talkin' like that, huh? Huh? Tell me that, you blunt-brained fool."

"Sleep?" Flemup stared back, astonished. "I can't barely keep my eyes open after all this watchin' we've had to do, but you sure better not think of sleepin'. No sooner as we close our eyes, and somethin's gonna eat us for sure! Don't you get it? Most all the dangerous stuff is huntin' at night, and it's well into night now."

Something moved in the brush just outside the firelight. The thieves' fury at each other instantly died away; they scooted closer, drawing their blades, and trying to focus their eyes into the dark.

A voice called to them. "Hello the fire! Can I come in?"

The thieves just nodded; stupid with fear and fatigue.

Elvodug's brain was feverishly measuring the situation. He'd kept himself alive all these years by figuring things out quick and then acting; he'd take chances as much as the next man, as long as there was a big enough reason for it, like that bag of silver the priest dangled before them, which they would get when they brought Suzie in. But that bag of silver's coveting influence was growing less weighty on the scale of his greed; his desire to live was tipping the scales toward flight.

The man in front of them added more to these feelings than the dark wilderness, dragons, and wolves could have done combined.

He came out from the trees, moving quick, almost menacing, like a panther might — confident, possibly stalking prey but not yet committed, proud and disinterested at the same time. In his left hand a large crossbow waved like an extension of his hand. Most men could not wield such a large weapon with one arm, but his sleeves were full to bursting with muscle, so that he carried it with ease.

In his right hand was a long bearded axe — this he held close to his leg; his pointer finger drummed softly on the shaft.

A hooded cloak kept his face hidden.

But the hood fell away with a slight shake of his head, revealing a square jaw, broad head, and a neck almost as thick. He gritted his teeth causing a rippling of muscles in his face; it reminded Elvodug of feral cats, wild animals with abnormally big jowls, enlarged by the perpetual crunching of bones and tearing of flesh. Even the man's eyes looked hungrily upon them.

But worst of all was the man's name and the reputation that came with it. Elvodug and Flemup knew of him, and had even seen him before, but they were always quick to leave the neighborhood of his presence. For he was a dangerous man-hunter who always got his prey — kinds like him stood out by the high quality weapons they carried even though they were not of the nobler classes. He was paid well for being so good at what he did.

It was Mortimer Blud.

"Elvodug … Flemup …" Blud said, lowering his crossbow in a more natural pose; yet doing so positioned it so that it was aimed very near to Elvodug's chest. "Are you planning on using those swords or are you inviting me to join you at your fire?"

The thieves sheathed their swords instantly. Elvodug's mind wasn't working just right under the watchful eye of Blud nor with that crossbow pointing at him — had he called them by their names? He knew them then, but how? Unless …

Elvodug gulped and tried to smile. "We'd be honored."

Blud's eyes narrowed.

That had been a dumb thing to say — honored — any fool could see that he was using a flattering tongue. It was just so hard to think; if only he'd turn that crossbow to pointing at something else.

"We were settin' ourselves up to have a little grub," Flemup said. "Welcome to join us if ya like."

"I'll eat later."

"Sure, just bein' hospitable." Flemup said, passing a piece of jerky to Elvodug. They chewed in silence.

Mortimer Blud dragged a fallen log closer to the fire and sat down. He took a big mass of leaves and twigs from where it had been tied to his back and set it gently on the ground before him. He patted it like it was a dog curled up at his feet.

Elvodug could feel Flemup's questioning eyes looking his way, but he didn't dare return the look. Something was mighty peculiar about this man-hunter. Elvodug's head was beginning to clear and his sense of self-preservation was telling him they needed to extricate themselves from this situation. But what if he was actually hunting them? The man's reputation spoke plainly enough — there was no getting away.

Then a thought occurred to him that relaxed him considerably. Who in their right mind would care at all about Flemup or himself? They certainly weren't worth the cost of hiring the likes of Mortimer Blud. Yes, that was plain fact, as plain as Flemup's face. In fact, if Blud spent the night at their camp, they'd be a lot safer, not much chance of something eating him.

With those comforting thoughts, Elvodug felt his tongue's fetters begin to loosen. "That's an interesting pack, you've got there." he said, and this time his smile was genuine.

"Yes."

"Looks kinda like a squirrel's nest?"

"It was."

Getting answers from Blud was starting to feel like pulling teeth. Flemup took a turn. "What ya do? Climb up a tree and steal it? Squirrel's make good eatin." Flemup laughed.

Mortimer Blud turned his head slowly towards him. Flemup's laugh died away; he couldn't bear up under Blud's stare; Flemup found something interesting to look at in the dirt. Elvodug felt some satisfaction at his fellow thief's discomfiture, while here he was having a pleasant conversation with the notorious man-hunter, and it was obvious to anyone that it was a conversation of equals.

He almost felt sorry for Flemup.

Elvodug would get the particulars himself; it was a curiosity — a man carrying a squirrel's nest on his back and then patting it like it was a pet. There was something weaved in amongst the nest that stood out … a bit of cloth … no, it was a piece of vellum, and there were some words on it, but Elvodug couldn't make them out.

"So, you carry a nest on your back. Don't see that everyday."

"No." Mortimer Blud smiled for the first time, but it wasn't a very comforting smile. He picked up the nest and slowly wiggled his hand inside. "I've got something in here."

Elvodug had a sudden change of heart. He no longer wanted to know what it was.

Blud kept his hand inside the nest as he shifted his gaze between them. "You two ask a lot of questions."

"Didn't mean anythin' by it. We were just curious, but not no more, man's got to have his secrets. Isn't that right Flemup?"

"That's right." Flemup's head was down, but he was looking at that nest out of the corner of his eye.

"Ever seen one of these?" Mortimer Blud pulled his hand out holding a small, round ball of fur. He rolled it along the log, snatched it right before it fell off, tossed it into the air, and caught it.

"A ball? Sure we've seen one before." Flemup said.

Mortimer Blud shook his head.

"It's not a livin' creature, is it?" Elvodug asked, when he saw Mortimer kind of petting it.

"It is."

"What kind of creature lets a man do that to him? That can't be no livin' …" Flemup's voice trailed off. He had just about stepped over a dangerous line, insinuating that Blud was a liar.

Mortimer didn't seem to notice. He suddenly got real talkative though. "This here is a 'sleepy one' better known as a dormouse. He can hibernate for as long as seven months. That's why I can roll him around and toss him in the air, and he won't wake up. As long as I don't hold him for too long, or his body temperature will rise, and he'll think it's time to wake.

"I found this squirrel nest in a fallen tree and thought it would make a good home for my traveling companion.

"You fellows look awfully tired, so you'll probably appreciate what I'm about to say. See, this dormouse makes a good pet, and he's usually quite sociable. But as the time for hibernating comes upon these critters, they're at risk, for whoever falls asleep first is in danger of being pounced upon and eaten by the rest — even its own mother. There's also the problem of sleeping too long. After six or seven months they wake up hungry, and let's just say, a few too many winks can prove deadly when the others are stirring.

"I see that I've disturbed you with my talk. I shouldn't have thought two men such as yourselves, braving the perils of the night as you are, would be bothered by a little thing like this 'sleepy one' — there goes my stomach rumbling, guess I'm more hungry than I thought. Getting tired too though, thanks for the hospitality. Being a solitary sort, I sometimes get hungry for other people."

Elvodug felt a chill go up his back. "Funny use of words," he said, laughing. Flemup wasn't even smiling. Neither was Mortimer Blud. "I mean, it kinda sounded like the dormouse talk, sounded funny like that."

Still Mortimer Blud didn't smile. "You want the first watch or shall I take it?"

"No, no," Elvodug said. He tried to sound natural, but he didn't feel like it was working. "We'd better let our food digest a little before turnin' in. We'll take the first watch."

"I'll just sleep in the brush over there, come wake me when you're tired. Just come in slow and easy, I don't want to mistake you for an enemy." Blud absentmindedly ran his fingers over his axe blade; he seemed to struggle with some hidden thoughts for a long time. Then he shrugged his shoulders. "Mighty hungry all of a sudden, almost thought I might have a bite first, but I'll enjoy my feeding time all the more come morning. Don't forget to wake me when you're tired."

He had only walked a few steps away when he suddenly turned. "I almost forgot. I'm tracking someone; a little girl, and the sign is mighty strange. If I'm reading it right, and I usually do. Someone tied her up in a bag, and then some giant badgers carried her away. Thought I'd mention it in case you two wanted to help me find her come morning, if you're still around."

As soon as Mortimer Blud disappeared into the woods, Flemup turned his intense, troubled eyes upon Elvodug. He spoke out of the corner of his mouth. "What are we gonna do?"

"Give me a second to think," Elvodug whispered. "And don't look so obvious."

"Obvious?" Flemup whispered back, with crazed urgency. "I'll tell you what's obvious. He's onto us, and I think he's gonna eat us. All that talk about his weird pet. You better think of somethin' and quick. I tell you I don't want to be eaten!"

"Would you quiet down!" Elvodug said, beginning to feel the panic himself. "We got a little stored away, what do you say to forgettin' this whole thing with Suzie, and settin' ourselves up somewhere else."

"You're a genius Elvodug. I tell you, you're a genius."

The Waiting Chamber

Fergus Leatherhead very nearly let his agitation show.

Ubaldo was resting in the adjoining chamber; and he would not be able to join them at the banquet, which was set to begin at any moment, for whenever he stood a dizziness came over him, and his head ached terribly.

Oded seemed uncommonly sad, and he had already wondered out loud, three times just this afternoon, 'Where is that little Suzie?' or 'What will Suzie think, me not coming to look for her?'. He was sitting in a corner, another heavy sigh working on Fergus's nerves.

Igi stood to the side of the door, angry red scars on his face and arms. He couldn't stop talking about how King Strongbow had taken their weapons and made them veritable prisoners. "Heroes' banquet indeed!" he began again, as he clenched and unclenched his fists. "Guards posted outside our doors! And what excuse does he give? That he can't have the giant Ogre armed at his table, no that wouldn't do. But he can't rightly insult him either … so what's his solution … take everyone's weapons. Agh! It makes me feel ill. I've never so much as slept without my sword since I was old enough to lift one."

Only one of the giants, Ogre, was well enough to come to the dinner. The flesh-tailor or sawbones, or as some people called him, the doctor, said he had four broken ribs — the slightest movement must have been unbearable, the pain severe. Fergus respected the kind of resolute strength it would take to come in spite of his nearly helpless condition, and he would be all alone amongst those whom he likely considered enemies.

The sawbones had to remove giant Lunace's arm, for it was shattered beyond mending. He would be weeks in recovering. And giant Goblin was dead.

Igi glared defiance from his post, like a cornered saber-tooth deprived of his fangs. It was strange to see him, usually so secure in his might, become so unsettled. He had been bested by the giants twice now; perhaps that weighed heavily on his mind … still, there was never any shame if one fell in battle to a superior foe.

Igi growled as if in response to Fergus's thoughts. "That Ogre won't even be able to lift his cup let alone a sword. And I'm in the service of a lady. How can I rightly protect her without my sword? Isn't there a law against taking a guardian's sword?"

No one said anything in response, though Mercy smiled at Igi Forkbeard, as if to reassure him that she had every confidence in his abilities.

To be fair, it was a dreadful feeling — to be without one's weapons, but the constant and angry lament from Igi was provoking. If there had been only one sword to use between them, Fergus would have gladly given it to him. It disturbed Fergus profoundly to see men agitated. Why could they not exercise self-restraint despite their feelings, like he had to do now amidst all these horrid displays of emotion?

Lord McDougal was staring distractedly out the open window, a peaceful smile on his face. Didn't this annoying talk get to him in some way? — no, he knew it did not.

Finally, Fergus could bare it no longer. Perhaps the right words, said in just the right way …"If the time came, Igi, that we should need weapons, and ours had not yet been returned to us—"

"Not returned!" Igi smashed one fist into his open palm, "How dare they!"

This exercise in self-control in the face of a man who was losing all semblance of control had a strangely restorative effect upon Fergus. "Yes. We all understand that it was an unjust act. We all feel it deeply—"

"Deeply?" Veins in Igi's forehead suddenly appeared where there had been no sign of them before. "You look as if you're talking about the weather, or this year's crops."

"Yes—"

"Yes!? Is that all you can say?" A wolverine in battle could not come nearer to the fierceness of Igi's appearance.

"Well . . ." Fergus felt his composure begin to slip. Just in time, he raised the thoughtful mask back upon his features. "I had a thought, Igi, would you like to hear it?"

"If it's a good one, I suppose then I do."

"If anything is planned against us, other men's swords should surely be forfeited to us, we shall take them. They will be confident; give them no reason to fear you, and they will most likely be over confident. But the way you look right now will have every guard within fifty paces nervously fingering his dagger.

"You could practice controlling yourself at once, while we yet wait. Make yourself look relaxed, and don't speak at all if you think your voice will betray you. Then if any one of us sense danger approaching we could use a code word, like the weather, or this year's crops, to be spoken aloud in natural conversation. That would let the rest of us know to be ready for instant action.

"Does that meet with your approval, Lord McDougal? What do you say, Igi?"

McDougal interrupted, "A town crier comes."

They hovered as close to the window as four large warriors could, while still making room for Lady Mercy to approach. The chamber was four stories up, but the street noise lessened to almost nothing, so that they had every hope of hearing the news.

The great bells of the city rang out ten times. The crowds gathered, and then the town crier bellowed his tidings:

Have the rumors reached your ears?
What does it mean that the witch Esla has died?
She sickened at the games, grew worse,
and passed with Lord McDougal's name upon her lips.
What does it mean that the Chronicler has disappeared,
with signs of a struggle within his chamber?
What does it mean that the king's mind is troubled?

He has brought you glory and exploits like no other kingdom.
He has given you the desires of your hearts.
The king loves his people.
The people's adoration lay like a pillow for Strongbow's head,
a salve for his soul,
a heavenly lifting up.

But something is wrong. What is wrong?
Have you seen the Dragon Priests among us?
Among them are those of the familiar spirits.
The king has sought their understanding,
and the Dragon's familiars have spoken:

The crier stared into the eyes of all those within his sights reach. Someone called out, "What did they say?" The crowd echoed the question with murmuring apprehension. The Crier pantomimed as if he were slowly drawing a hood up over his head.

They spoke thus:
The king is at a crossroads.
Birthed as a god, or haunted by the failed pangs of deity denied.
If a god, then his people shall see greatness,
If not a god, then there is a place for blame to fall …

Look no further than the God of Noah and the followers thereof!
King Strongbow's mind must be cleansed!
There must be a cleansing!

The town crier swung an imaginary cape before his face and ran through the amazed crowd. The cryptic words hung in the air, 'There must be a cleansing!'

Just then there was a knock at the door. They all started a little.

Lord McDougal smiled joyfully. "I wonder what God shall do with us tonight. The conversation should be stimulating … and the food … God has made the most amazing foods, I wonder if our cooks—"

The knocking was more insistent.

McDougal held out his arm for Lady Mercy. "Shall we go and see, my Lady … what great things God has planned?"

The Heroes' Banquet

"Truly," McDougal said, smiling his boyish grin, "this food is splendid! Taste and see that the Lord is good. I never cease to be amazed at all the flavors He has given us. Are you also enjoying yourself, my King? For this is grand hospitality you've shown us this evening."

The king sat at the head of a huge table, seventy cubits long, thronged with curious eyes, mustache's munching, and pale slender arms dabbing at the corners of red lips. "I'd rather not hear of this food or my hospitality, McDougal. This is the third time already, and I am attempting to speak with you of more weighty matters." The tone in Strongbow's voice was enough to stop McDougal's fork in midair.

"I apologize, my King, if I have vexed you. I'll just keep myself from certain dishes so that my heart shall not be so eager to speak forth praise; I shall stay away from the potatoes … and the venison. I'd better not have another bite of it … and I suppose the pie—"

Oded was eating his second piece of pie at that moment. "Mmmm … taste pie and see that God is very good! This is the best pie I've ever had."

Fergus winced. He couldn't help himself. He didn't want to be ashamed of Lord McDougal or Oded. But he was embarrassed by their uncouth behavior amongst the royals. He could see the knowing looks exchanged between Lady Catrina and some of the other nobles. Even the guards, standing watch over the meal, had trouble keeping their stoic faces.

Young Thiery carried himself in a more well-bred manner, and he just a foundling raised by Oded — of all people — and he dressed well … very well.

Fergus glanced towards Mercy. She was looking at him with a sad, imploring expression.

She knew what he had been thinking. She saw through him. He had let his emotions show on his face … had anyone else noticed. It was dreadful to contemplate.

Fergus' own thoughts had been read by the pure, sweet Mercy, and reflected back at his conscience. Exposed by her silent entreaty, Fergus flushed and looked down at his plate.

What an unfaithful wretch he was, a false friend and a treacherous servant. Worse yet, McDougal had appointed Fergus to keep an eye on Mercy, to be her companion for the evening — it would be unbearable now. He did not like it when others knew or suspected his weaknesses, but it was all the more difficult when the discovery came from someone close to his heart.

Was she still looking at him? Had her silent entreaty changed to disappointment and then displeasure? With an effort, Fergus lifted his head, and glanced her way. She had turned slightly, seemingly undisturbed, she was even smiling. To Fergus's mind, it was the greatest of kindnesses.

King Strongbow's voice inquired yet again, "Lord McDougal, I wish to hear the particulars of how you were able to defeat, in fair combat, the giant Goblin. Over and over it seemed, at least from where I sat, that his sword passed through your body, cleaved your head in two, struck off your leg, and yet somehow my eyes deceived me and you still stood. Instead, it was he all along who was receiving the wounds, until he fell over dead.

"Unbelievably, you had not a drop of blood on you. How is it so? I want an answer, and no more talk of food or hospitality. Did you gain some great powers while journeying with the dead? And if you try to tell me again that you were not dead, then I shall give Lady Mercy back to the Bacchus Priests." Until now, the king had seemed his normal self, but something came over him as he spoke, there was a darkening of his brow; his countenance became haunted and sinister, and then just as quickly it was gone.

The high priest of Bacchus looked up eagerly from his plate.

Fergus was suddenly alarmed. He began to pray fervently that God would give Lord McDougal wisdom.

McDougal's fork still hung in the air, a sumptuous taste of pie glistening before all. Fergus wanted to reach out and take it away. McDougal considered, looked at the morsel, and then slowly let his fork ease downward. Fergus let out his breath slowly.

"It happened very fast, my King. Indeed Goblin's sword over reached mine considerably, his strength more than twice my own. His armor, his skill ... what can I say, but the truth; If God be for me, who can be against me. But if God calls me home, than who can keep me here."

The king's eyes burned brightly. "Aha. I knew it. God gave you powers so that no man of this earth can hurt you. I knew it. I knew it ..." Strongbow studied McDougal intensely.

There was a look of deep sorrow upon McDougal's face as he looked about the room trying to speak to the guests with his eyes, that it was not true, that he was simply a man, that God was the one who deserved such wonder and fear — God alone! The threat to send Mercy back to the priests kept McDougal's mouth shut.

Fergus looked at each person as McDougal did. He saw unbelief in some, uncertainty in others, and a few who were persuaded as the king was; the most convinced of all was Ogre. His massive body towered over everyone, even Oded; all through the meal he had grimaced whenever he lifted his cup just as Igi had said he would, but still the guests eyed him with apprehension — he was a monster of unstoppable proportions, and indeed it was hard to imagine that a few broken ribs could hold back his wrath once it was awakened.

But Ogre watched McDougal now with his mouth hanging wide, completely unaware that it was yet stuffed full of food.

Strongbow was smiling again; he had gotten the answer he wanted. Now he turned his gaze, and fixed it upon Fergus.

"Fergus Leatherhead. You were lost to my eyes for most of the battle. Then, when all seemed at an end, you appeared from nowhere and won the day. I would like to hear, as would my guests, the winning of the battle firsthand. The Dwarven Brotherhood has not seen fit to return to me the hero Gimcrack, but we have you at least to tell the tale."

All eyes turned. They wanted a show. Any attempts at modesty might be misinterpreted — by the king at least — as offensive or obstinate conduct. McDougal could get away with it, but everyone knew that he had his eccentricities and that he was a lord.

Fergus was but a shield barer.

"Yes, my King. I will do my best. I saw an opportunity to throw my spear, and I took it. But I only slightly wounded Goblin, and angered him terribly —"

"No, no, that was plain enough, pick up when he struck you with his war hammer."

"Of course, my King. The blow stunned me, and knocked my sword from my hand. I hit the water and sunk. I don't know how long I lay on the bottom of the canal weighed down by my leather armor, but it could not have been too long. The desire to breathe came upon me, and then the desire to live, and then I was fully brought back to my senses, and with them, the desire to do my duty.

"Only, when I tried to swim, my right arm would not answer, it felt numb. But the water was not deep.

"I pushed with my legs to the surface nearest the fighting, so as to keep myself hidden alongside the canal's rim, praying that Goblin's sword would not await me.

"Some feeling was coming back into my arm, but there was no strength in it, and I could not pull myself out of the water. So, I half kicked, and half pulled my way along the canal towards the ship. When I finally reached it, the sounds of battle were ending, and I was worn out. I dared not call for help, for who knew if a giant would hear me first and find me helpless. So I rested and gained some strength, hidden well alongside the ship. I held onto a thick rope that reached into the water.

"I heard Lord McDougal speaking with Lunace about fearing God, and asking him to give up. My arm felt almost normal by then. I was catching my breath. Suddenly, the crowds were cheering. That could mean only one thing; that we had won.

"But then, there was an ominous quiet, broken by Ogre's voice. And I knew he had risen to battle despite his wounds — he who we thought had no more fight in him. And so I began to pull myself up the ship's rope. As yet, I did not know what had become of Lord McDougal, and then I heard Lunace calling to Ogre to get him out of the bog.

"Ogre answered that he couldn't, that it hurt even to breathe, and there was no way he could pull him out.

"Lunace growled something about his smashed arm, his own unbearable pain, and that Ogre better hurry and kill the dwarf before he bled to death.

"I heard a scuffling of feet, and when I came over the side I just caught a glimpse of Gimcrack jumping from the ship's rail like a berserker soaring through the air, wielding his axe and screaming. It made me proud to be his friend. Almost taken by surprise, Ogre swung his sword up in defense, and in so doing, he batted the head of Gimcrack with the flat of his blade.

"Ogre cried out in agony, not from any new wound, but from his broken ribs I suppose, and Gimcrack was knocked unconscious.

"Right away I saw the apparatus Gimcrack had configured on deck – Lord McDougal had instructed him to make it. I grabbed the boom and swiveled it hard. Ogre never knew what hit him. And that was it. I thank God, that that was it."

Ogre was no longer gaping at McDougal; he was now staring at Fergus, gritting his teeth loudly.

"Now that," King Strongbow said merrily, "was the grandest battle, to finish the grandest games we've ever had, and likely ever will …" His voice trailed off. He suddenly grew melancholy, and Fergus could hear him whispering, "If only there were more … I want more … my people want more … they love me." Then he murmered the last words that were still clear enough to understand, "… am I not a god?"

The king stared at his plate, moving food around, and muttering to himself.

A servant removed the candelabra closest to the king, leaving him in gloomy shadow, and carried the light down the table length toward the queen at the other end.

As the light brightened about the queen, and all eyes naturally followed, she began a conversation with a noble woman on her left. Princess Catrina followed suit with a young gallant. It was all that was needed to prompt the rest of the guests to start conversations of their own. The room began to buzz with excited chatter; only occasional glances toward the king betrayed the underlying current of foreboding in the hall.

Thiery sat only two chairs away from the king; a peculiar design, for every seat's occupant had been prearranged before they arrived. *Who was this boy to even be given a seat at all at the king's hearth?* Lord McDougal sat between him and the king. Lady Mercy sat opposite McDougal, and Fergus sat across from Thiery, followed by Igi Forkbeard and Oded. Next came two representatives for the missing heroes: Cnutfoot of Tump Barrows, standing in for Gimcrack, and a man introduced as the Green Archer, standing in for Count Rosencross.

Fergus studied the strange man, as did many of the people present.

Oddly, he was clothed in all green — spotless and richly embroidered; mysteriously he wore a green mask that covered his eyes and the top of his nose; and curiously, jagged scars, evenly matched, ran down both cheeks. He seemed to be indifferent to the stares of those around him, but Fergus noted that whenever Thiery moved the Green Archer's eyes were upon him, and when others looked at the boy, the Green Archer in turn watched them.

When first ushered into the hall, Thiery had just enough time to inform the heroes that he had left Suzie safe in a Dwarven Brotherhood's way station. And that he had seen Gimcrack, who was on his way to get her and bring her to the Chronicler's ship. Their conversation had then been interrupted, just as Cnutfoot was explaining a plan for secret flight, by not one ship only, but a fleet.

Fergus looked at Lord McDougal. He seemed to be enjoying himself, unmindful that this invitation was forced, that up till now, they were veritable prisoners, not guests.

McDougal put his arm around Thiery's shoulder. "Now that we've found you, or shall we say, God has brought us together, I wonder what we'll do with you."

Thiery grinned. "It feels good to be amongst so many friends. Suzie will be very happy."

Oded's grin was big and lopsided. Cnutfoot's eyes sparkled. Igi mumbled something about being careful, for Thiery was overly talkative, but no matter what the boy might say he wouldn't be driven to table busting by him; Igi too, was smiling.

But there were sinister looks as well; a Dragon Priest, with blue tattoos swirled about his bald head, stared at the boy. The priest suddenly laughed, seemingly at nothing, for no one was speaking to him or making a jest nearby. Then his face became animal like, and he appeared to be snarling. Fergus felt a chill go up his spine.

The high priest of Bacchus was having an animated conversation with the high priestess of the Queen of Heaven. 'Law of the Vestal' and 'she must die' could be heard by many sitting around them, and they dared to even point at Lady Mercy.

Of a sudden, Fergus thought he saw the countenance of Princess Catrina transform, for the most fleeting of moments, into a visage of hate. But it happened so fast that he was not entirely sure, and yet following her line of sight, he was disturbed still more, for it seemed that she too had been looking at Mercy.

This meal could not end quickly enough as far as Fergus was concerned.

"I almost forgot. Igi, this is for you." Thiery pulled a dragon claw from around his neck and handed it to Igi Forkbeard, as he did so, his own came out from under his shirt and displayed itself in full view upon his chest. "I followed the dragon the next day and she was dead. You fought her as well as I, so I got a claw for you."

The king was listening now.

He leaned forward in his chair, his hands shook. They stopped their quavering when he placed them down on either side of his plate. He leaned still more, over his food, tottering before the nearest candle. Out from the shadows the king had come. A lone candle sputtered and threatened to go out as he spoke through its flame.

"Who are you, boy?"

Counselors

"I'm called Thiery, my King."

Strongbow stared, perplexed.

"You invited me, I believe, after seeing me at the trial yesterday."

"The trial … yes … you're the æthling who was sacrificed to the Dragon?"

"Yes, my King."

"You claimed the God of Noah?"

"Yes, my King."

"And no other?"

"There is only one God, and Him I serve."

The king looked thoughtful. Fergus expected him to get angry; others at the table were showing signs of agitation. "After you were poisoned, did you go anywhere, see anything?"

"I passed out, my King, and I don't know exactly how long it was before I awoke. But I was in no shape to go anywhere. When I finally did get up, it was to the river. My throat hurt something terrible."

"No, no. I mean when you were dead or on the brink of

death, did you not pass over to the other side? What did you see? My father was buried with six beautiful horses, his favorite hound, great riches, servants. Did you see him? Was he a king there as he was here? Did his hound follow at his heels? Were his riches about him?

"Look at my counselors, the high priests of our gods. They tell me that they have seen these things when they peer beyond the veil. Did you see any of it? You are just a boy, yet you were courageous enough to speak your mind before the high-counselor, will you not speak to me now?"

Thiery did not hesitate. Though every man in there must have been thankful the same question had not been put to them — this young boy did not hesitate. "Where no counsel is, the people fall."

Strongbow had obviously not expected such a strange response, but the very peculiarity of it seemed to intrigue him. "Yes? I spoke of my counselors."

"Let not an evil speaker," Thiery said, calmly, "be established in the earth."

The king's eye's narrowed in thought. "To whom do you refer?"

Thiery answered, though not directly. "They hated knowledge, and did not choose the fear of the LORD."

"The fear of the LORD!" King Strongbow repeated. "Men are indeed fools if they do not fear the gods."

Thiery winced at the king's response. He continued, "Does not wisdom cry? The fear of the LORD is to hate evil: pride, and arrogancy, and the evil way, and the froward mouth, do I hate. Counsel is mine, and sound wisdom: I am understanding; I have strength. By me kings reign."

"Again I say," Strongbow said, his manner decidedly changed, "To whom do you refer with all this talk?"

"My King, the man that wandereth out of the way of understanding shall remain in the congregation of the dead. There is no wisdom nor understanding nor counsel against the LORD. Yet these counselors of yours have no fear of God, they abide in the congregation of the dead, and they seek to draw you there also. You are in danger of establishing evil men in the earth.

"They have lied to you about what they've seen beyond death. Your father could take nothing with him, for as he came forth of his mother's womb, naked shall he return to go as he came, and shall take nothing of his labor. They speak to you with doctrines of devils, to lure you away from the God who created you, and to whom we have to do, and give account. You must make ready to give account to your God, my King.

"I give you true counsel. I pray you'll heed it, though it comes from someone as young as myself."

There was silence in the room. It was obvious by the faces round about, that Thiery was fast becoming the smell of death to all those present who called not on the God of Noah.

It was terrifying and wonderful at the same time. Lord McDougal was on the edge of his seat, his face was shining as he listened to young Thiery speak of God — so boldly, so beautifully, as one who rested in God's faithfulness even as the jaws of death were clamping shut.

The king was startled. He sat back in his seat.

The Dragon Priest stood, and all eyes turned towards him. "He has said that we abide in the congregation of the dead, but by the laws of the Dragon, this boy is already dead himself.

"No doubt the God of Noah has aided him up till now, but he has called the rest of the pantheon, false gods, of which you are fast becoming one, my King. He has called us liars. You believe as we do. He has therefore called you a liar. Do you think the gods shall let him live much longer?

"We priests and followers of the gods, and especially you, my King, are the hands and arms of Bacchus, Marduk, the Queen of Heaven, the Dragon, and more. We shall clench god's fingers and wrest the life from this blasphemous youth, unless you would seize the honor yourself, my King."

Strongbow's eyes blazed to life. He looked into the faces of his subjects, and saw all that he needed, for Strongbow would be hard pressed to go against their wishes. "I will take the honor—"

The Green Archer stood. "My King, you love sport. Your people love the sport you give them, they love the tales, the poetry, and the skaldsong you inspire. Shall I continue?"

The king was turned by this praise as a ship by its rudder. He waved his hand to proceed.

"I will write ætheling Thiery's skaldsong, it is well composed already. His yarn's threads have been woven with yours. I have risen early and amassed the words; I will pile a hill of King's praise that will long endure without crumbling in poetry's field. The games are at an end, but something grander begins that will enshrine the King's immortal praise in verse.

"Shall we not give them more? Let us excite your subjects and extend the tale. Instead of killing the boy outright, why not a contest between Thiery and the long arm of these gods?

"Of course, we do not want to spoil this dinner, but we could arrange the particulars tomorrow at your convenience."

The Dragon Priest scowled. He was built like an ox. "I'd agree to this contest as long as we priests have a say in the planning, and as long as it involves driving a knife through his heart." This last, he said while pointing at the Green Archer.

The Green Archer smiled. "My King, if you are so inclined, I agree to the priest's terms, and I'll even give him his chance at my heart straight away. I could pepper him with blows, this priest of the Dragon, but for a brute such as he, it will only require one — one blow only." He raised his fist. "I will hit first with this, and I dare say it will not even leave a bruise upon that fearsome face. If he has recovered from my blow sufficiently then he will have to the count of ten to strike his knife through my heart. I will not move from my place for the full count of ten." He turned and looked at the priest awaiting him eagerly.

The king readily agreed to all the terms. Thiery was taken away between two guards. A space was cleared, and the two combatants faced one another. The Dragon Priest held a long dagger in his hand.

"Hold on tight to your weapon," the Green Archer said, grinning. "I'd hate for you to lose precious time hunting for it if I were to make you drop it." Yet, the Green Archer could not have weighed more than a hundred and thirty pounds, and the priest was well over two hundred. Could he really hit him hard enough to keep the priest from striking back within the ten seconds agreed upon?

The Green Archer held his fist up before the face of the priest.

He took a deep breath, opened his palm, and blew.

The priest cried out in agony, dropping his dagger, and rubbing desperately at his eyes. He fell back as if he truly had been struck with a powerful fist.

The crowd was counting. One, Two, Three.

Suddenly, the priest seemed to hear the numbers being called out. He tried to open his eyes, only to gasp in pain.

Four, five.

He dropped to his knees and searched blindly for his weapon. Amazingly, his hand hit upon it on the first try.

Six.

The priest jumped to his feet with a hideous howl.

Seven.

He tried to open his eyes, and gasped again. But his eyes were open long enough to turn him in the direction of his prey.

Eight.

The Green Archer stood still, eyes riveted to the priest only a few feet away. The priest, snarling, his blue tattoo's making him look like a fiend from hell, lunged forward with the blade. It narrowly missed.

Nine.

The priest swung wide to the left, missing again. He would not have missed if he had struck the other way.

Ten.

The guests gasped as the priest swung the dagger back to the right.

That strike would have killed or badly wounded the Green Archer, but now he could move, and not a moment too soon. Impossibly fast, he leapt back. The blade just caught his shirt, tearing it open, but no blood followed the cut.

Guards closed in on the priest and grappled with him before he could hurt any of the guests in his fury.

The Green Archer raised his open palm. "Pepper, my King. One blow of pepper." And then he bowed.

Princess

The king and his guests had been thoroughly entertained by this strange man. While they yet clapped, curious admirers surrounded him with praise and questions. They were enjoying the mystery of the masked man dressed in green. For the Green Archer was a known novelty, but a fleeting glimpse of him here and there throughout the city was all anyone could ever boast of, yet here he was, in the flesh, wooing them with his charms.

Fergus was glad that the Green Archer had taken all of the attention from McDougal's band, at least for now; he scanned the faces of the heroes whose banquet this was supposed to be; they were like lions and bears deprived of their cub — it was not easy to watch young Thiery taken away without lifting a hand — each had the look of the hunter in his eyes.

They looked to Lord McDougal. The muscles in his jaw rippled as he gritted his teeth, and then he cautioned them with a few words, "My friends, only a desperate man or a fool would bring in the crops just yet, and we are not so desperate."

The veins in Igi's neck seemed as if they might burst. His fists clenched and unclenched.

Lord McDougal smiled at him. "Igi. You'll agitate the hornet's nest, while your charge still sits in its midst."

Igi glanced at Lady Mercy from the corner of his eyes. She was watching him without a hint of reproof, but he turned scarlet from his neck to the roots of his hair and bowed his head.

"Crops and hornets?" Princess Catrina questioned, obviously enjoying McDougal's startled expression. "Shall I read conspiracy into these veiled words?"

"I … I did not see you there, Princess." McDougal bowed awkwardly. He bent so deeply, and his body was so long, that Catrina had to step back in order to save herself from a collision with his head.

"Lord McDougal," Catrina asserted with a snobbish air, "if you must fumble so, please give me fairer warning."

"I'm terribly sorry, Catrina."

Princess Catrina took another step back as if affronted. "Am I so familiar to you," she said with disgust, "that you forget my title."

It was too much for Fergus to bear. How could she treat him this way, especially in front of others? McDougal was a Lord, a guest of the king, a hero to all of Hradcanny — he had even been engaged to this horrible woman who now scorned him publicly. His only comfort was that there would be no chance now of that unwise union coming to be.

Lord McDougal was no match for her, neither were any of the powerful warriors who watched helplessly as she abused him. McDougal stooped towards her, with his gangly arms uncertain where to perch, his legs uncertain what position best to keep, and with an uncomfortable, embarrassed countenance. His friends averted their gazes. Princess Catrina reveled in her power.

But Fergus could not turn away. He stood straighter by his lord's side, for once he was not embarrassed, he only wanted McDougal to see that all was well with his faithful friend. So what if others might stare! So what if he stuttered at times! Fergus was his man through thick and thin, and he desperately wanted to let his master know it. He implored McDougal with silent thoughts, "I'm here, my Lord. I'm here."

Then Fergus saw a wonderful thing take place. The only thing really that could have turned the tide so forcibly.

Lord McDougal, of a sudden, was relieved of his discomfiture. His body, while still arched forward, no longer conveyed the posture of humiliation, but it now had the look of how an adult might stand when addressing a child who was much smaller than he.

His hands folded neatly before his belt. His legs ceased to move. And his eyes shined with a hint of wetness, his lips curved slightly down, his eyebrows creased softly together. It was the face of sadness — of pity.

In that moment Lord McDougal must have stopped caring so much about how he looked and what others must think of him — especially what Princess Catrina thought of him — and then he must have seen the princess as she really was: A lost young woman deceived by false gods, and deceived by her own heart; with a father mad for the pleasures of this world and a mind that was slipping from sanity; a girl, beautiful in appearance, with all the world adoring her, yet no character, no hope, no fear of God, no correction to keep her from herself.

Fergus saw Princess Catrina flinch, and then stick out her chin. "Lord McDougal," now there was no haughtiness in her voice, "may I speak with Lady Mercy on the Veranda?"

He bowed, this time only slightly. "You may, Princess Catrina … if Lady Mercy wishes it."

The princess stiffened.

"I would like it very much, my Lord. Princess Catrina is dear to my heart."

Catrina stiffened again.

Fergus followed, eager to keep Mercy close by him, afraid that even here, at the king's dinner party, someone might try to harm her.

There were a few others outside on the veranda, enjoying the cool night, and the views out over the city, views which were marvelously beautiful from the great height of New-Castle: the fields, the mountains, the valleys, and way off in the distance one could just see the glimmering moonlight upon the ocean.

As the princess and Lady Mercy stepped outside, those already there turned to see who it was and quickly left the veranda in silence.

"Do you see how those noble's left at once, Mercy? Deference to one's betters makes the world go round nicely. They saw by a look that I wished to be alone with you, and they simply floated away."

Fergus had not left, but had followed closely at their heels, and now Princess Catrina was looking up at him impatiently.

"Fergus," Mercy remarked, "I'm a little thirsty. Would you be so kind as to get me something?"

He had been prepared to keep his post no matter what Catrina might say or do, but now he was confused. Refusing to get Lady Mercy a drink seemed unreasonable. Lord McDougal, Oded, Cnutfoot and the Green Archer were all on hand. And Igi Forkbeard was watching not twenty paces away.

Yet, it was his special duty tonight to keep her safe. Fergus glanced over to the table. He could see Mercy's glass, half full.

"Fergus," Mercy chided him, "What could possibly happen within the few moments you retrieve my drink?"

"Yes, my Lady."

As Fergus turned away, he thought he glimpsed a look of malicious triumph on Princess Catrina's face, a look that set his heart to beating. He hurried his steps.

He picked up the glass and spun around. The high priest of Bacchus stood in his way.

"I have a question for you …" the priest began, but Fergus was not listening.

He looked past the priest and saw Princess Catrina standing at the veranda's parapet, pointing down into the city. Mercy was following her gaze and leaning somewhat over the edge.

The princess stepped back, and then back again, retreating quickly from Mercy's side.

"I said —" the priest was speaking again.

Fergus moved to go around him. The priest cut him off, and Fergus struck him down with one blow of his fist.

There was a familiar whistle. All conversations stopped. People stared at the fallen priest and at Fergus who was running towards Mercy. Guards drew swords. Then another sound chilled the blood of everyone present.

The thwumping of great leathery wings, a dragon in flight, its wailing cry piercing the night sky. Igi was running for her too. A few strides more and they'd have her safe again.

Mercy was straightening up, turning her head. He glimpsed her for a moment, her pale face filled with fear.

And then she was gone, her foot inches from his hand as she was borne into the air.

Fergus felt as if his heart would break.

He had failed … he had failed …

The great creature carried her away.

A Prisoner

An aerial view of Slowbelly Keep was quite beautiful.

It was small as far as castles were concerned; but huge and lonely as far as prisons were.

Four simple walls, twelve feet deep, sixty feet high, and two hundred feet long, formed a square. The walls housed a large courtyard and nothing else. On each corner of the square, the walls rose another story above the rest, but rotted timbers and roofing littered their floors, revealing the sky above. These corner buildings were the only dwelling places within the keep, and one must go through them in order to reach each adjoining wall.

From the ground, there were only three ways to attain the walls' parapets: climb scaling ladders, of which there were none; be dropped by a flying dragon, of which had occurred one week earlier with Lady Mercy; or climb up the only stairs, which ascended from the inner courtyard.

The only deterrent with the last, and wisest course, was a metal gate, barred but not locked, at the top of the stairs, and Slowbelly the dragon, of whom the keep was named. Slowbelly had free reign of the courtyard and stairs, but was kept from the parapets by the barred gate. The whole castle was like a giant cage, housing the dragon, while the walls' parapets were Lady Mercy's prison.

The keep was built atop the last great foothill of the mountains. The landscape sloped slowly away on all sides, especially towards the sea to the west, and towards Hradcanny to the east. One could stand along Slowbelly's parapets and see for miles; crags, rolling hills, and copses of trees dotted the landscape.

One stream of fresh, clear, delicious water flowed from a spring outside the keep.

Mercy could not help looking at that stream, so close, but impossibly far from her reach.

She was thirsty, but dared not drink any more of her own meager supply. An almost empty clay jug was at her feet. A squall that threatened from the sea might add some to it. Worse than her thirst, was the hunger. It was seven days since Squilby's terrible dragon had plucked her from New-Castle and carried her here.

Seven days without food.

Slowbelly hadn't eaten for a while either. On the third day after her arrival, Dragon Priests had marched up the path, leading a lamb.

Slowbelly had in fact acted as his name suggests; he seemed exceedingly fat and lazy, for all day he sunned himself, or at times he would crawl into what looked like a man-made earth berm at the center of the courtyard. Other than that he did not move … until the poor lamb was let in at the front gate.

Then the dragon displayed such speed and liveliness, which Mercy had previously thought impossible, that she stood transfixed, trembling. And all thoughts of escape were given up.

Slowbelly hadn't been fed since then, and he now made it a habit of climbing the long stairs, and peering at her from behind the gate. His eyes were dull, and he moved ever so slowly, but Mercy saw through the lumbering movements, and her hunger-dulled mind would sharpen into focus at these times, remembering what he had done before with the little lamb.

A thousand times she had cried out to God, wondering why she had to endure so much, asking Him to save her or bring her home quickly, asking Him to give her the strength to endure so that He would be glorified — asking for His strength to be made perfect in her weakness.

A thousand times she looked down the long valleys at a movement in the trees, or on a path, or on the sea, hoping that it was Lord McDougal, and Fergus, and Igi coming to her rescue. But each time her hopes would rise, and then fall, as the movement was only a waving branch, or a bird lifting to the air, or a beast traipsing through the fields.

The sun was just now warming the bricks she lay upon, and the chill she could not shake all night began to leave her. Then in the distance she saw another movement.

A bird? It grew larger. From the direction of Hradcanny it flew.

And then she could tell for sure that it was no bird, but that great winged beast. The dragon was coming for her again.

But she was too tired to move, and the sun felt so good. She would just close her eyes and wait.

Soon the leathery thrumping of its wings was too much, and even in her stupor, she felt the fear of it giving strength to her limbs. She opened her eyes and leaned heavily upon her arms, lifting her head to the sky.

The winged dragon carried a man. It was that wicked dwarf, Squilby. They hovered not ten feet away. The wind from the beast's wings made it difficult to see, for it sent her hair swirling about her face. If she had been standing, it certainly would have knocked her down.

There was a pouch in Squilby's hands. He said something and smiled at her, almost as if he were trying to be charming.

He dropped the pouch, saluted, and then whistled. The dragon banked its wings, soared higher, and then carried Squilby back the way he had come.

A snort startled her from behind. Slowbelly had climbed the stairs and was watching her from beyond the gate.

Mercy ignored him, crawled to the pouch, and opened it.

Inside were two biscuits, a crushed flower, and one of the parchments from which the town criers memorized their tidings.

With trembling fingers she raised one of the biscuits to her lips and with the other hand she raised the parchment:

By now the city rings with appellations;
Æthling Thiery, the foundling who baffles
and rebukes the gods;
his servant, Green Archer, the mysterious masked man;
and Lady Mercy, forced from the king's dinner,
by a shadowy flying beast!
These names, for sure,
are flowing from the tongues of Hradcanny's populace

News has recently come:
Lady Mercy has been carried away to Slowbelly Keep.

No doubt the gods are angry: A boy who mocks them;
their sacrifice stolen not once, but twice;
Dragon Priests made to look like fools, peppered with blows;
the high priest of Bacchus struck by a lowly shield barer.

The gods have spoken. How?

By sending winged dragon kind to ensnare her,
and earth bound dragon kind to guard her for the final contest.
Servants of the God of Noah versus the legion of gods.

The contest is simple enough:
One fair maiden awaits her execution.
Master Squilby and his flying beast
guard the paths that lead to her.
Slowbelly guards the gate.
The boaster of Noah's God, æthling Thiery, must set her free.

But there is more. Three hours after he departs,
a man hunt begins.
Æthling Thiery has been made a dragon's head.
On foot he travels.
Any may strike him down.
But an especial three shall take the chase:
Lunace 'One-Arm' and Ogre make the first,
Aramis, the huntsman, the second,
And Mortimer Blud, dreaded bounty hunter, the third.

Three hours again,
and the heroes of Hradcanny shall take to their heels,
The hunters shall in turn be hunted themselves:
Igi Forkbeard, Lord McDougal and Fergus Leatherhead,
Oded the Bear and Ubaldo the Silent,
the Green Archer and Cnutfuoot son of Redwald.

Come see people of Hradcanny,
for the leave takings begin tomorrow at dawn!

Mercy sighed. She laid her head upon the pouch to rest, before the cold night would make sleep impossible.

On Suzie's Path

Gimcrack sat before the dead gray coals which had once been someone's camp fire. Pip and Percival gathered wood to start a new one before dusk came upon them, and then covered them in forest-blackened night.

Count Rosencross sat opposite Gimcrack, his head down and weary, for he was not yet fully recovered from his sickness, and the day had been a long and arduous one, as they searched to find the trail. And find it they had; thanks to Snoot, the legendary dwarven-ranger — at least he was legendary among the dwarfs. He was still searching the grounds, with Horatio at his side, for further signs of Suzie or her captors. Soon he would return and tell them the story that the sign produced.

The trail sign was already a week old, but between Snoot and Horatio, and God's blessing, Gimcrack was confident they'd find her. They had to find her. Tomorrow began young Thiery's chase, and they wanted to lend a hand in whatever way they could, but first they must do their duty by Suzie. The plan was simply to find her, extricate her from the thieves who had stolen her away, and then bring her to safety; whether to the Chronicler's ship or one of the others which made up the fleet preparing to depart for a distant land. They would then be free to help the boy and Lady Mercy.

Count Rosencross had spoken little all day, and what words he had uttered, had only been doled out sparingly to little Percival. Whenever he looked at the boy, the Count's features would soften, and his words seemed less cold. Percival had been constantly by Rosencross's side during his sickness, telling him stories, feeding him when he was too weak to do it himself, cooling his brow with a damp cloth. Percival seemed to be utterly at ease with the scary man.

Gimcrack had always been afraid of him, with his black leather armor creaking as he strode through camp; his large muscular frame riding amongst his warriors and Dragon Priests, always on the verge of action; his eyes eager to explore, to hunt, or to fight.

But now, those eyes seemed haunted and his black gloved hands pulled at each other absently, as if he wished to rid himself of their constraints.

Gimcrack remembered what it was to be without God, and pity rose up in his bosom. He remembered also the torments that the Count went through during his sickness; the fevers, and the night-sweats, the moaning, and the troubled words that tore from his lips as he writhed upon his bed, and how one name seemed to calm him in his delirium.

Maybe it would be a comfort to him now.

Gimcrack swallowed hard and cleared his throat. "Count?"

His head lifted slowly. Two stony, bloodshot eyes, looked back at him.

Gimcrack was committed now, for he could think of nothing else to say; the only thing upon the tip of his tongue was what he first intended to ask. If only he could think of something, anything, for the Count's expressionless face was turning Gimcrack's stomach to rolling and flipping, and his heart to pounding.

"I was wondering who Johanna is?" Gimcrack asked. There, he said it. He got it out just barely before his voice began to quake. Would it have the same peaceful effect it had when Rosencross had whispered the name himself?

The Count's face hardened. "Who spoke of her to you?"

It wasn't working. In fact, he looked more dangerous than he ever had before. Gimcrack managed to squeeze out the monosyllable, "You."

"What?"

And then Gimcrack blurted it out in one continuous breath, "You did, sir, while you were twisting about with fever. Whenever you spoke her name, you'd calm right down, and a peaceful sleep would come over you for a while. I thought hearing her name again just now might be pleasant for you. I didn't mean any harm by it. I wanted to be of service to you, a help is all, that's all."

"What else did I say during my fevers?"

The first thing that popped into Gimcrack's mind, was the very thing he thought it most unwise to tell, but once again, the Count's fixed stare was making it hard for Gimcrack to think of anything else. It was as if his mind were too frightened to move, and there was only one little window by which Gimcrack could look into his mind's thoughts. And only one thought stared back at him. Should he speak of it? He could see the suspicion crossing the Count's features.

It was no use, he must tell him exactly what he saw in that little window of his mind, or Rosencross would know that he was hiding something, and that seemed a much more dangerous thing.

His eye twitched.

"Um, well, one night something kind of strange occurred."

"Yes."

"At the time, it scared me something terrible," Gimcrack said, tiny little breaths of air shaking his chest as he spoke. "Though, now I know it must have been my imagination.

"I was half asleep myself you see and I heard you talking to someone. You were angry, but I didn't pay it too much attention, for you'd been mumbling and such for a while, and like I said, I was dead weary tired.

"But then I heard someone else's voice respond back to you …"

Something changed in the Count's face just then that caused Gimcrack's tongue to stick. It was akin to fear, but the kind of fear that causes a wild cornered animal to fight its fiercest.

The Count's face changed again as he mastered himself. "Continue."

Gimcrack's dread was clamping down hard upon his nerves. He tore his gaze away from Rosencross. His eyes alighted on the nearest thing at hand, a magpie was flying about the camp. It landed and picked at something on the ground. Gimcrack remembered his God at that moment and sent up a prayer — imagining it as a bird in flight toward heaven. Maybe the Count would notice the interesting bird, and forget their conversation.

"Tell me!" Rosencross commanded.

Gimcrack could only obey, his limbs felt unsteady. "I don't know exactly what the voice said, but it was something about Thiery and Suzie, and Dragon Priests, and I think they wanted the children to die …

"You got angry again. The other voice said he was their father. You said he couldn't have them, you said …" The words hung up in Gimcrack's throat.

"Yes?"

"You said, that they were yours now. But I must have imagined the other voice or dreamt it."

"Why?"

"Because I lit a lamp as fast as my fumbling fingers could do so, and there was no one in the chamber. I searched it. I heard no footsteps walking away. You settled back down and slept, and then I noticed the wolf. Horatio had not moved. He wasn't even disturbed. If a stranger had been in that room, he would have growled at least."

The Count tugged mindlessly at his gloves as he stared beyond Gimcrack into the growing darkness, a faraway look in his eyes. One of the gloves came almost half way off revealing a myriad of small blue serpents tattooed on the back of his hand. The marks looked a lot like the tattoos that twined about the Dragon Priests' faces and arms. The glove was suddenly jerked back into place.

Rosencross was staring at Gimcrack now, and Gimcrack didn't like the look at all.

Magpie

Gimcrack had half expected that night to be his last, for Rosencross turned in without a word. His hand rested alarmingly upon his dagger. Gimcrack's imagination kept him jumping at every sound.

But in the morning he was still alive and Rosencross was actually pleasant with everyone. Pip and Percival noticed the change in his countenance immediately and reacted to it with their characteristic energy and excitement for life.

Truly, there was much to be excited about. Snoot and Horatio had taken them many leagues and he was able to tell them somewhat of Suzie's trail sign story, some of which they had known from the previous day.

Two men had taken her, lowered her over Hradcanny's walls, and then promptly lost her to a clan of wild badger, of the giant variety. The thieves had followed the trail until dark, camped, and then they were met by a third man, a large man.

In the morning, the first two men made off in the direction of Old City, and the third man — now on horseback — followed the trail which led to the badger clan's den.

By some means he managed to entice the clan to battle. He fled. They chased. And he simply rode around them, and carried off the girl. Snoot couldn't be for sure at first, for her weight was not considerable enough to change the horse's tracks much; but Snoot thought he saw the slightest difference.

At noon, he was certain, for the horse and riders had stopped by a creek, and had something to eat. There were now two sets of human foot prints, and one was that of a child.

Hopes were high.

During their own mid-day meal, Gimcrack was talking with Pip and Percival about his wonderment concerning their friend Thiery. He told them how the boy had such a stalwart faith in God, and how he had, over and over again, helped Gimcrack to turn from the precipice of fear towards the strong tower of God's strength.

Count Rosencross looked towards Gimcrack. "Why do you think he is like that?"

"Like what, sir?" Gimcrack asked.

"Like all those things you said about him. Most men haven't half those qualities, and he's just a boy."

"I'll tell you, Count, and I'll try to be as bold as he would be, though I don't know if you'll like it."

"I like boldness." Rosencross declared.

"God, for certain. It is God who's done it." Gimcrack began. The sun was warm; his belly content; the boy's eyes were large and earnest; Horatio was sleeping comfortably at his feet; Snoot was nodding his head in agreement; and even the Count seemed as if he genuinely wanted to know. All this freed the tongue of timid Gimcrack so that he told more than he ever intended, for it is easy for man to speak of the thing he knows and likes best — himself.

But that is what made the day so grand, for God was about to do a grand thing indeed, with lowly Gimcrack, who soon began to talk of himself. His thoughts went something like this: 'If I show myself the fallen sinner I am, saved by God's grace, then maybe Count Rosencross, will look at himself, repent, and find God's grace too.'

Gimcrack prayed and then took a deep breath. "You see, Thiery is a good boy, and he's been trained to know God and His ways, and he seeks God with all his heart, mind and soul. I, on the other hand have all my past mistakes and sins behind me, to drag at me.

"I've shown myself a coward to my Dwarven Brotherhood — I was often afraid. I'm still afraid of a few things here and there. Men have not always thought so well of me.

"In fact, when Lord McDougal wanted to take me into the Hilltop Inn, I felt the shame terribly for my fear would not let me go with him. The Dragon Priests were in there. I would never change. Still McDougal graciously left me at a post outside the Inn and he said they would come for me at noon.

"I thought that maybe I could make up for my disgrace. I left a note, and ran off to find my good friend Staffsmitten, a man I knew that McDougal would be only too glad to have on our side … even in that I failed.

"I did not find Staffsmitten, nor did I make it back by noon. Then, when I found myself face to face with Lord McDougal before the games began, he said that he forgave me for running away that night … he never found my note though he searched for me, even with Oded the Bear, and he a ranger.

"I saw his disbelief when I told him about the note and what I had tried to do. He quickly covered it and said, 'Well, I've got you at my side now and that is all that matters.' I could really see that he chose to believe in me, that he somehow believed I'd be solid through and through this time. It was amazing to me that he would trust me under the circumstances. If only he had found that note, and then he could have known for sure that I told the truth … ah well.

"'Then I failed poor Staffsmitten when the Dragon Priests took him away. I fainted from fear, and now he's dead. And then I failed Suzie. I wasn't there to protect her when she needed me …"

Gimcrack was beginning to feel quite low. He glanced occasionally at Rosencross, expecting to see his disgust. Yet it wasn't there. The Count was thinking, that was easy to see. Who knew what his own past hid, what things tormented his soul? It seemed likely that the Count's thoughts were rummaging in that direction, and his next question, and the way he said it, confirmed Gimcrack's suspicions.

"You've described things," Rosencross said, "that many a warrior would fall on his own sword for. How do you keep on?"

"Thiery told me that I must forget and never forget."

"Don't speak in riddles."

"Let's see … He said to forget that which is behind and press on to the high calling of God. So that I can bear fruit for Him, otherwise man soon finds himself self condemned, afraid to call upon his God, failing in his sins again and again, becoming enslaved to them, unable to see the grace of God before him, and his heart becomes hardened.

"But with God, His mercies are new every morning and His Grace is sufficient for my needs. So that by being quick to repentance, by knowing, yes, even growing in His grace and knowledge, I can run quickly back to His strong tower."

"But you said not to forget?"

"Yes, forget my past sins, but do not forget from where I've fallen. This is the state of every man. It is the state of depravity that each man must come to understand he has, before he can come to His God with humility. A man must think himself sick before he will go to the physician. Ever since Adam and Eve ate of the forbidden fruit, Adam's race has been dead. We've fallen and we must never forget from where we've fallen.

"You see, fallen man, in his pride, either thinks he has not fallen at all or that he can lift himself up, by himself, and make himself righteous on his own merits.

"If we do not show fruit as followers of God then it is because we have forgotten this truth; we've become blind and we cannot see afar off. That is the thing we should never forget. We were fallen men destined for hell, but by God's grace we do not have to go there, if we but repent and follow Him, not according to our ways, but according to His."

"And Thiery told you all these things?" Rosencross asked.

"Mostly him, though I did pick up some, here and there, from Staffsmitten through the years. Though from him, I would not listen over much. Thiery is one of God's loresmen if I ever saw one. He loves God's Word and speaks God's truth. He even memorized the Book of Job. But, he does not just keep God's Word at his mind's fingertips, he believes every word, and he lives by them — God's loresman indeed."

"So you think then that God has extended this grace to you, even after what you have done? All your cowardice?" Rosencross questioned, clearly doubtful.

"Yes," Gimcrack said, his voice was hushed and his head held low. He was not forgetting that which was behind, and the Count's question seared it upon his memory. He couldn't look at anyone. He imagined that even the boys were disgusted with him. If only he had said nothing.

Suddenly, a magpie was fluttering before Gimcrack, as if he were speaking to him. Not with words that he could understand, but nevertheless it hovered just above his head and chirped and twittered until even the Count was looking at it wonderingly. It could not make its normal sounds for there was a large scrap of vellum in its beak.

Gimcrack reached up slowly.

The strange thought in his mind was that possibly God was giving him a message by this extraordinary means. Hope, that this was so, filled his breast with heart thumping and belly flipping.

Before he could reach the scrap, the bird opened its beak and flew away. The vellum dropped softly at Gimcrack's feet. The side facing up had a dirty but distinctive image of a mountain on it, like one would find on a map. Gimcrack recognized it at once. He turned it over and read it aloud:

I am sorry that I have played the coward. Wish to make amends; off to bring reinforcements. Back by noon. Hope for forgiveness and your grace upon me. Your humble servant, Gimcrack.

Gimcrack had forgotten just what he had written, especially the sentence about forgiveness and grace. He stared down at it amazed. But he was even more amazed when he looked up and saw the rest of the party staring at him as if they had just witnessed someone raised to life.

Count Rosencross was especially awed by what he had just seen. And for the next three hours he said nothing at all as the trail brought them closer to the sea.

They crested a small hill. Beyond it was a cove, draped by tall trees on every side, and a thin egress leading out to the sea. There were six ships at anchor.

The largest ship was also the closest. There were sailors and warriors on board, and there were families too, many women and children. On the upper deck, a group of girls were playing, their laughter carried easily to the little party on shore.

Unmistakable, even at this distance, was a small wisp of a girl, hop-skipping among them, clapping her hands and giggling.

It was Suzie.

Superstitious

Fergus had watched the two giants, Lunace 'One-Arm' and Ogre, make their way across the rocks and walk into the stream, then walk a few hundred yards before leaving the cold water to make camp. They were careful not to leave any tracks.

They picked a place to bed down with their backs to an alcove in a rocky hillside. Their camp was well situated; for they could watch their back trail, and it was a good place to defend, being slightly higher than the approach before it. They were more than cautious, in fact, they were decidedly uneasy.

Neither said much as they opened their packs and removed their cold dinners. They were either too tired to start a fire, or they were wary of drawing unwanted guests to its warmth. They looked gloomily toward the stream.

The sun was less than an hour from setting and it was getting cold. The beauty of the early evening sun, glowing red on the trees, was fading as shadows now moved among them.

The giants suddenly stiffened and ceased from all movement, even their chewing. Coming down their back trail, was Lord McDougal, dressed in all white with a thin translucent cape flowing over his shoulders. He was carrying a shiny metal bird cage that caught the sun's rays and reflected it in a twirling pattern of what looked like tiny stars bursting into life and then dying and then bursting again as he walked towards the stream. He held the cage with great gentleness as though it contained something of remarkable value.

Following behind McDougal was Wooly, the mammoth, with Griz, the bear, riding atop him. Wooly let out a powerful trumpet blast.

Fergus had always enjoyed this time of day; he loved how God's creation took on an almost painted effect, somewhat surreal or dreamlike.

The giants were transfixed.

McDougal could be seen speaking to the cage, though his voice did not carry far enough to know what he said. The conversation continued for a few minutes, when he dropped his chin to his chest, as if he were sad or suddenly very tired.

When he lifted his head, he turned and looked towards the alcove; from where the giants sat watching the strange spectacle, a mouthful of food still not swallowed in each man's mouth.

Lord McDougal walked slowly across the stretch of land between them. He followed the stream's edge. Wooly and Griz stayed upon the rocks and watched him go.

He had barely begun, when a terrifying howl came from the forest that paralleled the stream and McDougal's path. If Fergus hadn't known that the originator of that howl was Oded, the sound would certainly have sent shivers up his neck.

The giants flinched, but McDougal appeared not to even notice. Then a faint drumming sound could be heard from the same direction of the howl. It was approaching closer and louder towards the forest edge.

Lord McDougal did not so much as turn his head. He came on as if he were in a dream, peaceful, but intent upon the alcove where the giants waited.

An arrow flew from the woods, and thudded into the dirt before McDougal's feet.

He kept on.

Another arrow, and then another, until Fergus lost count due to the number and speed of their appearing.

The flowing white form of Lord McDougal with the shinning prize which he carried simply strode through the flight of arrows as if he were an angel traveling in the heavens, unable to be touched by things of this earth.

Arrows struck trees, stream, rocks, and dirt, but nary a one hit Lord McDougal. Though some looked as if they passed right through him, at least one could imagine such a thing. Fergus thought that the giants certainly did as he watched their reaction from his hiding place.

The arrows ceased, as did the drumming and strange howling from within the forest's depths. Wooly and Griz were gone. But McDougal still came on.

Lunace came to his feet suddenly, his sword in hand, "Stand Ogre, we must meet him on our feet."

They were massive, powerfully built giants, awaiting a lone man. Even Lunace, without his arm, would be a terrible foe to meet any warrior in battle, but with Ogre beside him, it seemed entirely foolish to approach as McDougal was. Yet, they must be dealt with. They sought to capture Thiery, and they would not hesitate to bring him in dead.

So the hunters had been hunted. Now that they had found them, what would the giants do?

McDougal stopped a few cubits from their reach and said nothing.

The giants looked back with ugly stares. Then Ogre pointed at McDougal's cape as it unfurled in the breeze. There were ragged holes along its length, suggesting that arrows had passed through, yet there were no holes in McDougal, no traces of blood.

The giants glanced behind them. They must have realized that the camp they had chosen so carefully, had become a cage from which they could not escape, unless they went through Lord McDougal. They did not seem inclined to move in that direction.

Lunace 'One-Arm' nodded his head solemnly.

"Lord McDougal 'the dead'," he began, "You are a great warrior among your people. You have killed Goblin when no one else could. You spoke to your god, I mocked him, and then my arm was gone. You defeated us in battle, you strung us from trees as if we were children.

"We had never known fear before you came to us. We know fear now, but we are not cowards. We will fight even though our blades pass through nothing, and your blade cuts us in two. Yet, we are bewildered; we do not understand your ways. Your sword is sheathed, your hands are empty of weapons. We see the talking bird in that cage. Will it turn into some terrible beast and fight for you?"

McDougal smiled his boyish grin. "Lunace and Ogre, it is you who are great warriors, among your people and ours. Your names cause fear in the breast of every man among our realm. But it is God whom I fear above all men. It is Him who brings me to stand before you now, and of whom I wish that you also would fear, for the fear of God will keep you from evil.

"I am here not to do battle, unless you force my hand, but to ask of you a boon, and to give you a gift in return."

Until now there was a sad, knowing look upon the giants' faces that portended only doom for themselves. Suddenly there was a glimpse of hope, most evident in Ogre's features.

"What boon do you ask for?" Lunace asked suspiciously.

"Only that you leave off this hunt, and let young Thiery go."

"We would return to our lands in the north with nothing then but shame, and the loss of one of our greatest warriors."

"No, you would return with your lives, and with this talking bird. You would be its keepers. You would bring to your people something very valuable."

Greed and alarm both played across the giants' faces. "Will it speak with us?"

"Try it. Birdie does not always speak on command, but ask it if it is hungry."

Lunace was quiet.

Ogre spoke up eagerly, "Can I Lunace, can I be the one to ask?"

"No," Lunace growled. "It is a great thing. I must be the first."

Ogre's lip snarled a bit, but he held his tongue.

"Great Birdie of the shiny cage. Great Birdie that speaks as a man, and flies through the air as no man can. We humble ourselves before you Great Birdie and ask that you would speak with us. I am Lunace 'One-Arm', this is Ogre. We are great giants among the giants, but we are nothing compared to you, Great Birdie.

"Are you hungry, Birdie?"

The forest itself seemed hushed, McDougal's eyebrows were raised, and Ogre's mouth hung open.

"Food, eat food." Birdie called out clear and true. Fergus thought that never had more happy words been spoken.

Lunace puffed out his massive chest, and a huge grin stretched his dreadful face wide. "Birdie has spoken. Ogre, get him food. We are the great keepers of Birdie!"

Mercy's View

It was midday, or a little past. Mercy strained to keep her eyes focused. The brick upon the ramparts were warm again. Weakness and sleep were calling her to lay her head down. Last night had been so very cold.

But she dared not sleep just yet, for a moment earlier she thought she had seen something way off in the distance; maybe a person running on foot, between two rocky crags. But nothing had emerged on either side, and she wondered if she were seeing things. She felt as though she would cry, as if she could take it no longer. Her emotions were strung up tight as the cordage on the Chronicler's ship … the Chronicler's ship … those were happy days, oh, to be back on that ship, with her friends by her side.

I don't know how much more I can take, my God. Please help me to be strong. Where is the boy? Will he come? Please, please keep him safe. Will you send my heroes, your valiant men, to save me. I think it would be a very beautiful thing, but your will be done, always Lord, your will be done.

There he was. It was a man, or more likely a boy. It was far, but she thought that she could almost recognize him. It was Thiery, it had to be him. And he was drawing near. The thrill was almost too much. Her pulse quickened, her mind sharpened, and she stood straight — that is what almost sent her reeling — for she was very weak. Holding tight to the parapet walls, she watched as he, ever so carefully, with his body close to the ground, made his way from stone to tree to crag, when suddenly he froze.

The boy couldn't see his danger, but Mercy could, though he must have heard something. A man on horseback came from the trees trotting his horse perpendicular to where Thiery lay. In a moment, the rider would have him in his sights, and there would be little hope left.

Thiery's arm suddenly swung up and then back down. Mercy could imagine a rock thrown, but she could not see something so small. The rider looked sharply in the direction to where the stone landed.

Just as he turned his horse away, Thiery was up and running. Like a deer he bounded over the rocks, and through the grass, trying to make for the relative safety of some woods, about three acres round. Beyond them was a small meadow and then a larger copse of trees, with jutting rocks bordering its far side. She could see that he might get away if he could hide himself amongst those angry crags.

But the rider had been little fooled and wheeled his horse in chase. She could hear the thundering hooves in her mind, though all she could know of it, from this distance, was the turf, and rock, and dust that flew from under the charger's hooves.

The boy made the first woods with little time to spare. The rider pulled up hard and listened. As quick as lightning his horse was off again, racing around to the meadow on the far side. But he had hesitated too long, for faster than it seemed possible, the boy broke from the first wood, and was running headlong for the second.

Then the rider gave his horse its reigns, and it showed its true worth, for it sailed across the rock strewn grassland as if it were an ethereal ship-steed riding the yellow grassy-waves, full sail before a tempest wind. It was a prince among horses, or possibly a king.

She wanted to turn away, to not see the poor noble youth ridden down, but she could not even close her eyes, so mesmerized was she by the sight. Just maybe, just maybe … *Oh God, could he not live?*

The horseman was gaining fast, but then Thiery was a prince among boys, and as fleet a foot as ever a man could be. He glanced back once, and then his previous rapid pace seemed to be a friendly lope compared to the swiftness which bore him on next. No man can outrun a horse, unless God were to make it so, but the boy did move with what seemed to Mercy supernatural speed, and just fast enough to make the wood.

The horseman was not to be hindered so easily. Reaching the woods a moment behind Thiery, he vaulted from the saddle and took after the boy on foot. It seemed an eternity as the chase continued hidden from her sight. She prayed fervently for Thiery's safety.

After a long while, the pursuer exited the wood and climbed onto his charger's back, empty handed. The rider was lost to view as he rode behind the copse. At the same moment, Mercy caught a movement way up in the treetops.

Thiery was there, carefully climbing from tree to tree, occasionally stopping to listen, and then he would move swiftly again amongst the branches, as if he had been born to that lofty world of hawks and squirrels.

He might come to her within the hour, and her heroes might not be far behind, for they would have ridden hard to intercept him. She thanked God with all her heart, and then her heart almost stopped.

There was still a good amount of ground for the boy to cover before he could get to her, and the land was such that most paths would eventually lead through a larger grove, which grew only a few hundred feet from Slowbelly Keep. One wide lane snaked through to its heart and then out again almost to the keep's portcullis. The forest's heart itself was a grassy glade with a pile of rocks at its center — a heart of stone — which at that moment pulsed with Dragon Priests, their red robes spilling about the clearing.

Squilby's dragon stalked among them, muzzled, yet fearsome. Squilby led the creature by a leash.

He turned and looked up at her, a flower in his hand.

He raised the red bloom to Lady Mercy and waved.

The Red Rose

Thiery had wondered who he was, and the mystery surrounding himself, ever since he could remember. This intensified when his own father, a Dragon Priest, tried to have him killed. It now seemed amazing that he could potentially have, upon his person, the beginnings of a thread which might unravel the mystery. What was more amazing still, was that he had the letter, given to him by Diego Dandolo, for more than a week now, and he still had not read its contents.

First, they had been interrupted within the Green Archer's room by Cnutfoot and Gimcrack. There had not been a moment to spare because of planning or there had been others about, all the way up until the heroes' dinner. Well, there had been one moment, but Diego was not present, and knowing how much it meant to him, Thiery had been reluctant to open the letter without him.

Thiery then had a whole week to ponder its contents while he waited for the dragons-head hunt to begin. Almost every night he dreamed that he had opened the letter, but for some reason or other he could not see what it said. He would wake to realize that it was only a dream. And his waking hours of that week had been spent in a dungeon, a dungeon with only the hint of light, nothing by which one could read.

When the hunt began, again there was no time. It would have been selfishness to look upon that parchment while Lady Mercy was waiting to be rescued and when the heroes of Hradcanny were counting on him. When he had stopped to rest the night before, again it was too dark to read, and a fire was out of the question. All he knew of its contents were what Diego Dandolo had read, 'My Dear Grandfather …' It was very little to go on. Had his own father or mother penned those words?

Thiery stopped moving amongst the tree tops and wondered if he should climb down now and run for the rocky ground, which he knew he could hide himself in. Or should he keep to these trees, hoping the rider and the other huntsman would not discover his whereabouts. He did not need to get much closer today. He knew it would be dangerous and perhaps foolish to dash for Slowbelly Keep at this hour, with the huntsman so close at hand, for Squilby was the greatest danger on this side of the keep's portcullis, and he was likely nearby. As of yet, Thiery had seen no sign of him.

If he did not move, the chances of being seen were less. If he waited, then his friends might soon come. And there was Slowbelly the dragon to deal with once inside the keep. Wouldn't it be wise to let Oded and Ubaldo fight that creature, for what could Thiery possibly do against something so formidable. Then again, it was God who Thiery must put his hope in, and God could do anything, even slay a dragon with a boy's hand. That is exactly what God had done before. Would He do it again for young Thiery?

Still, it seemed wise to wait for his friends; it was they who were the heroes of Hradcanny. And if he was going to wait, then would it be so terrible to read the letter which hung from his neck, under his shirt in a small leather pouch?

Some sudden danger might cause him to lose the letter forever. After a moment he decided to risk it.

Then a scream changed his mind.

From where he sat in the trees he could see Slowbelly Keep, but not well, for he had moved away from the forest's perimeter, afraid that one of the huntsmen might see him.

Still, what he did see caused the blood to rise in his face; he clenched his teeth and began descending at once, even as he watched.

Lady Mercy, wearing the same white dress from the king's dinner, was running along the keep's parapets, her grey robe streamed behind her. She was running for one of the corner guard rooms. Squilby's dragon was giving chase from the air.

She hadn't a chance. The beast plucked her from the walls and flew out over the countryside. But Mercy did not give in so easily. She fought and managed to break free with one arm. Thiery gasped, thinking of what would happen to her if she got completely free, so far up in the air.

The dragon was losing control and so dipped into the wooded grove before the keep. As soon as they were out of sight, there was another scream and then silence. Had she fallen?

Thiery dropped to the forest floor, saw nothing in the intervening distance between he and the woods where Mercy and the dragon were, and left all to God's providence and care as he shot from the woods, running up hill through the rocky grassland before him.

He thought of His God as his heart pounded, *'Fear before Him, all the earth. Let the heavens be glad, and let the earth rejoice: and let men say among the nations, The LORD reigneth. Let the sea roar, and the fullness thereof: let the fields rejoice, and all that is therein. Then shall the trees of the wood sing out at the presence of the LORD.*

'Save us, O God of our salvation, and gather us together, and deliver us from the heathen, that we may give thanks to thy holy name, and glory in thy praise.'

Thiery made it to the woods safely. No alarm went up, no cry of attack, no wailing dragon scream … nothing. He was almost through to the middle of the forest, when he saw that it was thinning out suddenly, a clearing was opening before him, and it was terribly quiet, deathly quiet …

A part of him was uncertain, as if trying to tell him that something was not right, to get away quickly. But then, he saw in the heart of the clearing, a pile of rocks, and on it, as if she had fallen from the sky, was Lady Mercy.

Her grey cloak covered most of her body, her long brown hair covered her face, an arm was outstretched before her; and in that hand she held a red rose.

Hope welled up inside Thiery's breast. For if she were dead, would she still cling to that flower. He saw nothing in the sky, but the dragon might return.

All Thiery had to do, was run out and touch her, and at least according to the rules, he would have accomplished the quest set before him. He would have rescued her without even having to encounter Slowbelly.

Thiery put it to the swiftness of his feet and God's protection to bring him to her in safety. He realized too, that Squilby's flying dragon would not understand that the hunt was over, and so Thiery might have to carry Lady Mercy back into the forest where the dragon's wings would have trouble following.

He ran hard and in seconds he was by her side. Still there was no movement among the trees, and no stirring of leathery wings upon the wind. Yet, something did not feel right. Thiery's heart pounded and his stomach flipped at the uneasy feeling, but there was no time to think, only to act.

He reached for Lady Mercy to lift her up, when suddenly Lady Mercy herself grasped one, and then the other of Thiery's arms, with a vice like grip that must have been born of fear. The rose dropped to the ground.

Then Lady Mercy began to laugh. A laugh that put dread into Thiery's soul.

It was an evil laugh.

The long brown hair fell away, slipping between two rocks, and the triumphant, twisted face of Squilby with his bulging eye came up out of the white dress and grey cape, and stared inches away from Thiery's face.

Mercy was not here at all. Thiery had fallen into their trap.

Dragon Priests, nearly fifty of them, carrying crossbows, filed out from two points in the woods and spread in a circle around the glen.

One man sat on horseback. Thiery knew him to be Aramis, the huntsman.

Squilby whistled. It was the same sound that Thiery had heard the night Lady Mercy was carried away by the dragon. Then Squilby released Thiery, "Run boy, see if you can get away."

Before Thiery had taken two steps, he was hit hard from behind, but instead of falling, he was borne into the air. The dragon had him. With an effort it began to lift him higher until Squilby whistled again.

The dragon let go, and Thiery fell ten feet to the rocks below. Nothing seemed broken. He got unsteadily to his feet.

"Just be glad," Squilby said, laughing, "that my Princess is muzzled. I can see it in her eyes. She's hungry and you look like a good meal to her. But first I'd like to see from what heights you can fall and still get back up again. Isn't it glorious, boy, to fly through the air?"

Squilby found himself so humorous he could not whistle at first, and then his laughter was interrupted by the loud snort of a horse.

All eyes turned to see Mortimer Blud upon his war charger, the one that had nearly run Thiery down earlier. "I'll take the boy." His voice was quiet but firm.

Squilby turned on him, menacing. "You? I caught him. He's mine. And what of Aramis, and these Dragon Priests, do you plan on taking the boy from all of us?"

"Yes." Mortimer gestured at the priests. "You've broken the rules — the priests were not part of the hunt. And he's led me quite a chase. I'd not give him up to the likes of you even if you had taken him yourself. I've never hunted a man that's gotten away. Never."

Squilby laughed again, pushing his eye so that it almost popped from its socket. He looked more intently at Mortimer Blud. "I wanted to see you better before you died. Priests, kill him."

A score of them pointed their weapons, without hesitating, and pulled their triggers.

Mortimer Blud was moving even before Squilby gave the command. He slipped off his horse, swatting him in the rear as he dashed into the woods. The bolts hit nothing but leaf and tree. Two priests writhed upon the ground, wounded or dying by Mortimer's flashing swords — one in each hand — skillfully wielded as he ran past.

There was true fear on Squilby's face now. If Mortimer Blud escaped alive, then Squilby's life would be in great peril. Squilby screamed, spittle flying from his mouth, "Get him! Get him!"

Thiery turned to run. But a whistle brought the dragon in an instant, and Thiery was carried up again. This time, he was twenty feet high when the dragon let go. Amazingly, he felt only bruised, but he was slow to rise.

"You don't die easy." Squilby said, approvingly. Then his attention was once again directed toward the woods.

There were yells and screams and then the rushing red robes, amongst the trees, were retreating. They flooded back into the clearing and began to reload their crossbows in a panic. The priests, who had stayed behind, turned their crossbows upon the forest.

The noise from the wood was still exceedingly loud. Some priests had not retreated and they were clashing with something large. There was ferocious growling, and trumpeting, and men's battle cries.

The false screams of Squilby, when he had pretended to be Lady Mercy, had been compelling. It was not only Thiery's noble heart that had refused to be cautioned at that cry. Squilby's trap had worked only too well, drawing into its jaws more than he could handle.

Griz and Wooly burst into the clearing, and were instantly engulfed in a rain of crossbow bolts. They faltered for an instant, and then tore through the priests, enraged by the multitude of stinging barbs that would see those loyal beasts dead before the hour. Oded, Ubaldo, Lord McDougal, Fergus Leatherhead, Igi Forkbeard, the Green Archer and Cnutfoot followed behind. From the opposite side rushed Count Rosencross with Gimcrack and Snoot close in the rear.

This time, when Squilby whistled, the dragon scooped Squilby into the air, just as Thiery whirled with his dagger. He had intended to attack its claw when the dragon came for him, but instead he threw it hard, and saw it sink deep into the dragon's wing. Squilby disappeared over the trees.

Aramis yelled McDougal's name, and the two clashed with such force that the combatants around them were forced to fall away. It was impossible to tell whose sword was whose as the two men fought. The two warriors were a blur of movement, flashing and clanging metal, and occasionally there was a glimpse of blood. Then more blood. Then they slowed.

At the same moment, they both toppled to the earth.

Thiery turned to run for the keep. He heard Fergus yell, "To McDougal, To McDougal."

But there was not time to see more.

A Dragon Priest finished loading his weapon, his tattooed head looked up at Thiery. Thiery drew his short sword and ran at him. As the Dragon Priest lifted his crossbow, Thiery knew that the priest would fire before he could bring his sword within reach.

Just then, Count Rosencross appeared before him, knocking Thiery to the ground. The Count jerked suddenly, and then cried out in a rage as he swung his sword. The red robed Dragon Priest crumpled before him.

Thiery looked, expecting to see a bolt sticking from the Count's body, but there was nothing.

Rosencross' eyes were aflame. "To the keep!"

He led the way at a run, with Thiery right behind him, and Gimcrack and Snoot guarding his flanks.

They paused at the portcullis for only a moment. Count Rosencross studied the layout. They could see Slowbelly watching lazily from a mound in the center of the keep's grounds.

"We must hurry." Rosencross said, his breath coming in short, pained gasps. "Gimcrack and Snoot you run to the stairs with Thiery. If Slowbelly gets past me before you've made it to the top. It will be up to you to stop it. Thiery, you save your mother."

"Mother?" That was not possible. Mercy was not yet twenty years old.

The Count's eyes were still fiery, but they seemed distant too, as if he were looking past them all. "Do you argue, son? Your mother needs you!"

"Yes, sir." Then Thiery saw the stain of blood on the Count's side. He had been hit by the priest's bolt, only it had been at such close range that it passed clear through him.

Together, Gimcrack and Snoot raised the portcullis, enough for them all to pass under, and then let it down with a thud and the sound of clanking chains, hidden somewhere in the portcullis' workings.

Before Thiery had reached the bottom of the stairs, Count Rosencross and Slowbelly were battling for their lives. When Thiery reached the top of the stairs and turned back to glimpse what was happening, Slowbelly was dead and Count Rosencross lay unmoving in a growing pool of crimson.

Thiery wrenched his eyes away, and put his arm through the bars of the gate to unlatch it. As he did so, he scanned the parapet walls for any sign of Mercy. He was afraid that Squilby might have arrived before them, and that Mercy would be gone.

But she was not gone.

She sat very still, leaning against the parapets. Her hands and feet were tied.

"My poor, Princess," Squilby cooed.

He caressed the dragon's head and carefully removed her muzzle.

"I know, my Princess, I made you wear this for too long. I've never seen you so upset."

Squilby's heart suddenly started to beat hard. He hadn't thought about how hungry Princess must be by now. They always listened better when they were hungry. But it had been days. He shouldn't have removed the muzzle until he had something for her to eat.

"Princess, my Princess," he cooed again. "Does that nasty dagger hurt? Let me help you, my Princess."

He made a movement towards the dagger, embedded in her wing, but she lifted it from his reach.

She was looking at him. Squilby's heart beat harder still. Should he run? No, never, then he would lose his control over this beautiful beast.

"Are you hungry, my Princess, Master Squilby will get you food. We must only wait —"

But, Princess did not want to wait any longer.

The wicked shall fall by his own wickedness.
He that pursueth evil pursueth it to his own death.

Theiry's Father

Lord McDougal and Count Rosencross were badly wounded, yet both lived. One stretcher was constructed large enough for the two of them to share. Oded and Ubaldo easily carried the burden between them.

The others had either slight injuries or no injuries at all. Griz and Wooly had borne the brunt of the battle at its outset. They died before night came.

Mercy was very weak. She was given Mortimer Blud's horse to ride. Gimcrack corroborated Blud's story, that he had found Suzie and brought her to the ships, and Diego Dandolo explained that he was indeed, despite his dangerous reputation, one of Thiery's guardians. Moreover, Mortimer Blud, or Redhand as Diego called him, had long ago been one of the boys, along with Diego, that the Chronicler had shown special attention towards.

The party of adventurers, worn and wounded, made it to the ships by midnight. The dawn brought favorable winds, so that the fleet slipped from Strongbow's kingdom, and sailed for new lands, yet unknown, where they might begin again.

Lord McDougal's health improved with each passing day at sea.

Count Rosencross worsened. He was conscious though, and he found much comfort from Lady Mercy, Suzie, Percival and even Gimcrack's visits. Thiery tried to see him, but after the first awkward interview, he was gently told that his presence was too much for the Count just yet. Surprisingly, it was Diego Dandolo who Rosencross would not be without, and so, Diego stayed dutifully by his side.

Thiery waited near the sick cabin, with Horatio, hoping he would be called in again. One week into their journey, Gimcrack came out, after one of his visits, and shut the door. Thiery looked up expectantly.

Gimcrack sighed. "Sorry, my boy, he's not ready."

Thiery looked down, pulling Horatio's soft body to his.

"He talks about you," Gimcrack said, a huskiness in his voice. "He wants to know all about you, the things you've done, and the things you say. He especially wants to know about how you walk with your God."

Thiery didn't dare speak.

The next morning Diego Dandolo was waiting for Thiery when he and Horatio came to take their post. Thiery's heart felt like it was in his throat, and once again he couldn't speak, for he was afraid that the Count was dead. Why else would Diego have left him?

"It's not what you think, young Lord," Diego said, smiling gently. "He has come to a crisis. I don't think he will live much longer. I read him the letter from your mother. He did not deny anything. His tears were so hard and bitter that his wounds broke open. He told me of all the evil that he has done.

"He wants to see you now, but I think he has never faced anything that scares him more. Before you go in, he would like you to know everything, but he cannot bear to tell you himself, so the task has been left to me.

"Your mother's letter explains much. Your father did have his sons, Belfry, Clovis and Arsuf sacrificed to the Dragon. He sanctioned their murder, and the guilt of it wrenched his conscience. After, he could not stand to see the purity of your mother, and so she too was sacrificed. For a time he was driven mad. When he surfaced from his delirium, he had changed even more.

"As his sin blackened his heart and seared his conscience, he became the Dragon Priest, yet he could not bear to look upon himself as such, and so he became two men. One man, the Count, had yet a flicker of hope and conscience still in his breast, and the second man, the priest, desired to be free from God and His laws, and so, Count Rosencross became a slave to sin and to the prince of the air.

"Together, they, or I suppose I should say he, sacrificed many others, and with each one, he carved a tattoo of a serpent upon his hands. Whenever he acted as Rosencross he wore gloves to hide the identity of the priest from others, but especially from himself. It was a terrible thing.

"You grew up in his realm, without him ever seeing you. Oded became your guardian when you were seven. Oded had never seen your brothers. He had no idea that you looked very similar to Belfry, your oldest brother. When the Count saw you one day, in the streets of Banockburn, he became suspicious. Then he found out that you were a foundling, and no one knew from where you had come. He looked into matters further and found out the truth.

"So it was, that you were sacrificed next. When you lay in your tent, sick from the poison, Count Rosencross spoke with a priest which you believed to be your father. When in truth, Count Rosencross was speaking with himself. Even changing his voice to that of a nasally priest, so complete was his own self deception.

"But God sent his loresmen, bearers of His truth, to chase your father down and shine God's glorious Word upon him. Lord McDougal, Fergus, Suzie, Oded, Ubaldo, Mercy, Igi, the Chronicler, myself and yourself, Gimcrack and even Pip and Percival were bearers of that light. We trusted not to ourselves, but to God's redemptive power.

"Your father is no longer deceived, Thiery. He knows his own wickedness. He has repented before God and men. And when you enter his room, you will see that he no longer wears the gloves.

"He and I have read through the Book of Job six times. He listens to Suzie sing of God and his face shines. He believes that the LORD will save even him, a worshipper of false gods, a murderer of his own wife and children, and a hater of the one true God.

"We have taught him this truth these many days as his body has grown closer to death, but he yet fears to see you.

"Are you ready?"

"Yes." Thiery's heart pounded.

Diego opened the door. Thiery stepped in. A small window was open and the sea lapped softly at the ship's side.

The Count was so gaunt and pale that Thiery could barely recognize him.

"Hello, Father."

"Hello, Son."

Thiery didn't mean to, but his eyes glanced down at the Count's hands.

"Do they disgust you?" Rosencross asked softly. His eyes seemed to want to retreat, to pull themselves away, but they did not; as if they hungered even more to see Thiery's response.

"No, Father."

"Words, only words. I see for myself." The Count's face darkened and twisted in pain, whether from his wounds or a heavy heart Thiery couldn't tell.

"No, I am overwhelmed, but it is not with disgust."

"What then, why do you look so?"

"Diego tells me that you have repented and seek God with your whole heart, mind, soul and strength."

"I have … and you think it too little, too late?" His voice was a whisper and his eyes were wretched. He stared in horror at the marks upon his hands.

"No, Father. We have sinned, and have committed iniquity, and have done wickedly, and have rebelled. To us belongeth confusion of face, to our kings, to our princes, and to our fathers, because we have sinned.

"But, to the Lord our God belong mercies and forgiveness, though we have rebelled against Him. Father, we can cry to our God and say: 'We do not present our supplications before Thee for our righteousnesses, but for Thy great mercies. O Lord, hear; O Lord, forgive; O Lord, hearken and do, defer not, for thine own sake, O my God: for thy people are called by thy name.'"

"My hands, Thiery, look at my hands!" His voice was shaking, yet his face betrayed his heart — he desperately wanted to believe his son's words.

"Your hands, Father, show the mercy and grace of God to the multitudes of sinners. I shall raise you and your hands up before my children and my children's children as an Ebeneezer, shining forth God's grace."

And so they spoke one to another. Count Rosencross had less and less to say. His eyes grew dim, and finally they closed.

And Thiery continued to speak of the glorious ways of God.

That night, father and son held hands. Once, near the end, Rosencross squeezed feebly. A last breath was barely audible as Thiery watched his father's now peaceful face.

The trouble of this world passed away from Count Rosencross of Banockburn as he entered into the Kingdom of God.

The angels sang.

For even a chief among sinners can find God's grace.

Epilogue

Keeping a secret on board a ship is difficult.

So it was that Suzie had heard a good many things about Lady Mercy. Sometimes from Mercy's own lips, but sometimes the news came from others — for walls were thin and privacy was scarce and fleeting.

The things she had heard had not been good.

It seemed most people were of the opinion that their new colony, when it was founded, must flourish quickly — they must multiply. In order to do so, the unmarried must get married.

And many of the single men among the ships were eager to make Lady Mercy their wife. So far, two ships of the fleet had sent messengers to Lord McDougal — for he was her chief protector and guardian — with five requests asking for her hand. All five had been denied.

That was the good part. The bad part, was that there were more men who would try soon enough.

At least the men on board their ship had not gotten up the nerve to even speak with her. For Lady Mercy was not giving encouragement to anyone. But how long would it be, before some handsome, dashing, and godly man was able to gain her affections.

Even Suzie could see that Lord McDougal was not exactly handsome or dashing — oh, but he was godly, and she was sure that he was much more so than any other man alive.

Suzie had quickly grown to love Lady Mercy and she desperately wanted her to be her mother. She also loved Lord McDougal and she desperately wanted him to be her father. If they did get married, but didn't think to ask Suzie about adoption, then Suzie would just give a wonderfully obvious hint.

Thiery thought the plan was a good one, and was on hand to help in any way he could, especially reminding her to pray and let God's will be done.

The difficulty was — and they had both noticed it — that Lady Mercy and Lord McDougal seemed almost not to like each other. They were civil, of course, but they were always hurrying to get away from each others' company, no matter how hard Suzie and Thiery tried to bring them together.

Lady Mercy was reading a book aloud to Suzie in the largest room of the ship, the captain's quarters, which had been fitted out for the women's lodgings. There were seven ladies who shared the space, and it was rare that Suzie ever got to be alone with Mercy because of it, as she was now.

Suzie put her hand gently on Mercy's sleeve.

Mercy stopped reading and looked up, alarmed. "I did not think the tale was as distressing as that, Suzie. Why, you look as if you might cry."

"Lady Mercy?" Suzie asked, suddenly afraid to speak, but feeling she must.

"Yes, child."

"Do you love me?"

Mercy pulled her into her arms, "Of course, child. Who could not love you? And I think I must love you more than anyone."

"Do you love Thiery, too?"

Mercy laughed. "Yes, Suzie. He is my champion after all, and he is your brother."

"Do you love Lord McDougal?"

Mercy's face at once turned pale, and then flushed red. Suzie could feel her trembling.

"Are you sick, Lady Mercy? Are you hurt?" Suzie cried, caressing Mercy's hair and cheek and arms in a frantic display of affection.

"No, no … I'm alright, child, you just … I just wasn't prepared—"

There was a knock at the door.

Mercy began straightening the hair that Suzie had innocently thrown into disarray. Suzie ran to the door and threw it open.

Lord McDougal stood in the doorway with Fergus Leatherhead. McDougal wasn't exactly standing, it was more like a deep bow, or like someone stretching to touch their toes. For he was so tall, and the ceiling of the chamber so low — for most ships, by necessity, must make careful use of their space, almost universally lowering their ceilings so that the average man must watch his head or bump it. McDougal had to either walk with his fingers trailing along the floor, or crawl upon it. Even walking on his knees caused his head to knock into the massive beams above.

The sight always made Suzie giggle.

"We were just talking about you, Lord McDougal," Suzie exclaimed with perfect joy. "Weren't we, Lady Mercy?"

Again Mercy's face burst into crimson.

Suzie saw it at once, and turned to McDougal, worried. "I think she might be sick, that's the second time she has turned all red, only this time she looks worse."

Mercy stood quickly with a look of dread upon her face.

"She's swooning!" Suzie blurted. "Catch her, Lord McDougal, quick, get her!"

It was a terrible place for Lord McDougal to be gallant in, which Suzie could see at once, for he could barely move himself within the ship's confining timbers, let alone hurry to someone's aid. He dropped onto his hands and knees, and scurried forward to catch the fainting Lady Mercy. Only, she did not fall. She just turned slowly around and then buried her face in her hands and cried.

Fergus still stood in the doorway, clearly unsure of what to do.

Lord McDougal looked very sad as his hands wandered about the air, touching the ceiling, then the floor, then his beard, and so on for the duration of Mercy's tears.

When she stopped, and only sniffled a little, the rest of the room was quiet. Suzie had an uncomfortable feeling that somehow, for she could not figure it out at all, but somehow, this strange scene had actually been caused by herself and not by some perplexing sickness, so that Suzie was afraid to even move.

Finally, Lady Mercy spoke without turning around. "Are you still hear, Lord McDougal?"

"I am. I'm at your service." He was still on his knees, but his head was bent sideways in order to fit under the low ceiling.

After another long silence she spoke again. "Have you come for a reason?"

"Yes, yes, forgive me, I had forgotten. Another messenger has just come with a letter addressed to me … that is, it concerns you, though it was addressed to me, an offer of marriage you see — not me, not my marriage. Oh dear, the way I just said that made it sound like I was given an offer of marriage, umm, it concerns an offer of marriage to you, not to me."

Suzie saw that the sickness was spreading very quickly, for Lord McDougal's face was growing red also.

She turned to Fergus Leatherhead, imploring tears in her eyes. "Can't you do something, Sir Fergus? Please."

Fergus seemed alarmed at first by this request, but then his strong and noble face returned to its confident bearing. He went to McDougal and whispered something in his ear.

McDougal looked confused and then spoke again. "Lady Mercy, there are actually two requests for your hand in marriage."

Mercy kept her back to him, though she was not crying any more.

Fergus whispered again to McDougal.

"The second request," McDougal said, "is from a man of great rank and godly heritage."

McDougal leaned towards Fergus to hear the rest of the message. His eyes suddenly went wide, he gulped, and his hands began to fumble in every direction once again.

Just then, Mercy turned around. She was composed though very pale. Her eyebrows rose slightly.

Lord McDougal froze. He now looked frightened. This was a very strange sickness.

"Would you possibly," McDougal began, he spoke very slowly, "consider marrying me?"

Suzie held her breath, and still she wasn't completely sure if she had heard him right, for he spoke so softly. It was a very confusing thing for a little girl like Suzie. Mercy started to tremble and cry again, but she was also smiling, and it was a very big smile.

What did it mean?

Then Suzie saw that Fergus was smiling, and she already knew from experience that he didn't do that very often. Lord McDougal was smiling too. Everyone seemed to be better. God must have healed them.

Suzie looked up towards heaven and smiled at God, for she was accustomed to praying and watching with thanksgiving.

When the fleet of ships reached land two weeks later, Lord McDougal and his wife Lady Mercy went ashore with their four children: Thiery, Pip, Percival, and Suzie.

The foundlings were foundlings no more.

"It is good that thou shouldest take hold of this; yea, also from this withdraw not thine hand: for he that feareth God shall come forth of them all." Ecclesiastes 7:18

Magic

Magic: The art of producing effects by superhuman means, sorcery, enchantment.
(From Webster's Dictionary and Roget's Thesaurus)

Magic: 1. The art that purports to control or forecast natural events, effects, or forces by involving the supernatural. 2. The practice of using charms, spells, or rituals to attempt to produce supernatural effects or to control events in nature. Synonyms: sorcery, witchcraft, necromancy.
(From The American Heritage Dictionary)

Isaiah 47:9-14

But these two things shall come to thee in a moment in one day, the loss of children, and widowhood: they shall come upon thee in their perfection for the multitude of thy **sorceries**, and for the great abundance of thine **enchantments**.

For thou hast trusted in thy wickedness: thou hast said, None seeth me. Thy wisdom and thy knowledge, it hath perverted thee; and thou hast said in thine heart, I am, and none else beside me.

Therefore shall evil come upon thee; thou shalt not know from whence it riseth: and mischief shall fall upon thee; thou shalt not be able to put it off: and desolation shall come upon thee suddenly, which thou shalt not know.

Stand now with thine **enchantments**, and with the multitude of thy **sorceries**, wherein thou hast laboured from thy youth; if so be thou shalt be able to profit, if so be thou mayest prevail.
Thou art wearied in the multitude of thy counsels. Let now the **astrologers**, the **stargazers**, the **monthly prognosticators**, stand up, and save thee from these things that shall come upon thee.
Behold, they shall be as stubble; the fire shall burn them; they shall not deliver themselves from the power of the flame: there shall not be a coal to warm at, nor fire to sit before it.
Thus shall they be unto thee with whom thou hast laboured, even thy merchants, from thy youth: they shall wander every one to his quarter; none shall save thee.

Malachi 3:5-6

And I will come near to you to judgment; and I will be a swift witness against the **sorcerers**, and against the adulterers, and against false swearers, and against those that oppress the hireling in his wages, the widow, and the fatherless, and that turn aside the stranger from his right, and fear not me, saith the Lord of hosts.
For I am the Lord, I change not

Revelation 9:21

Neither repented they of their murders, nor of their **sorceries**, nor of their fornication, nor of their thefts.

Acts 19:18-20

And many that believed came, and confessed, and shewed their deeds.

Many of them also which used **curious arts** brought their books together, and burned them before all men: and they counted the price of them, and found it fifty thousand pieces of silver.

So mightily grew the word of God and prevailed.

(Curious arts = magic/sorceries)

Revelation 21:7-8

He that overcometh shall inherit all things; and I will be his God, and he shall be my son.

But the fearful, and unbelieving, and abominable, and murderers, and whoremongers, and **sorcerers**, and idolaters, and all liars, shall have their part in the lake which burneth with fire and brimstone: which is the second death.

Revelation 22:14-15

Blessed are they that do his commandments, that they may have right to the tree of life, and may enter in through the gates into the city.

For without are dogs, and **sorcerers**, and whoremongers, and murderers, and idolaters, and whosoever loveth and maketh a lie.

1 Samuel 15:23-24

For rebellion is as the **sin of witchcraft**, and stubbornness is as iniquity and idolatry. Because thou hast rejected the word of the Lord, he hath also rejected thee from being king.

And Saul said unto Samuel, I have sinned: for I have transgressed the commandment of the Lord, and thy words: because I feared the people, and obeyed their voice.

Leviticus 19:26,31

Ye shall not eat any thing with the blood: neither shall ye use **enchantment**, nor **observe times** …
Regard not them that have **familiar spirits**, neither seek after **wizards**, to be defiled by them: I am the Lord your God.

Leviticus 20:6

And the soul that turneth after such as have **familiar spirits**, and after **wizards**, to go a whoring after them, I will even set my face against that soul, and will cut him off from among his people.

Deuteronomy 18:9-14

When thou art come into the land which the Lord thy God giveth thee, thou shalt not learn to do after the abominations of those nations.
There shall not be found among you any one that maketh his son or his daughter to pass through the fire, or that useth **divination**, or an **observer of times**, or an **enchanter**, or a **witch**.
Or a **charmer**, or a **consulter with familiar spirits**, or a **wizard**, or a **necromancer**.
For all that do these things are an abomination unto the Lord: and because of these abominations the Lord thy God doth drive them out from before thee.
Thou shalt be perfect with the Lord thy God.

For these nations, which thou shalt possess, hearkened unto **observers of times**, and unto **diviners**: but as for thee, the Lord thy God hath not suffered thee so to do.
The Lord thy God will raise up unto thee a Prophet from the midst of thee, of thy brethren, like unto me; unto him ye shall hearken;
According to all that thou desiredst of the Lord thy God in Horeb in the day of the assembly, saying, Let me not hear again the voice of the Lord my God, neither let me see this great fire any more, that I die not.
And the Lord said unto me, They have well spoken that which they have spoken.
I will raise them up a Prophet from among their brethren, like unto thee, and will put my words in his mouth; and he shall speak unto them all that I shall command him.
And it shall come to pass, that whosoever will not hearken unto my words which he shall speak in my name, I will require it of him.
But the prophet, which shall presume to speak a word in my name, which I have not commanded him to speak, or that shall speak in the name of other gods, even that prophet shall die.
And if thou say in thine heart, How shall we know the word which the Lord hath not spoken?
When a prophet speaketh in the name of the Lord, if the thing follow not, nor come to pass, that is the thing which the Lord hath not spoken, but the prophet hath spoken it presumptuously: thou shalt not be afraid of him.

Keepers of the Word

Kept (Strong's #5083) = *Tereo* (as in Rev. 3:8) a watch, guard, hold fast, keep, preserve
Keep (Strong's #8104) = *Shamar* (as in Psalms 12:7) to hedge about (as with thorns); to guard, to protect, attend to

Revelation 1:3

Blessed is he that readeth, and they that hear the words of this prophecy, and **keep(5083)** those things which are written therein: for the time is at hand.

Revelation 1:9

I John, who also am your brother, and companion in tribulation, and in the kingdom and patience of Jesus Christ, was in the isle that is called Patmos, for the word of God, and for the testimony of Jesus Christ.

Revelation 3:8

I know thy works: behold, I have set before thee an open door, and no man can shut it: for thou hast a little strength, and hast **kept(5083)** my word, and hast not denied my name.

Revelation 6:9

… I saw under the altar the souls of them that were slain for the word of God, and for the testimony which they held:

Revelation 22:7

Behold, I come quickly: blessed is he that **keepeth(5083)** the sayings of the prophecy of this book.

Revelation 22:18-19

For I testify unto every man that heareth the words of the prophecy of this book, If any man shall add unto these things, God shall add unto him the plagues that are written in this book:
And if any man shall take away from the words of the book of this prophecy, God shall take away his part out of the book of life, and out of the holy city, and from the things which are written in this book.

Psalms 12:6-7

The words of the Lord are pure words: as silver tried in a furnace of earth, purified seven times.
Thou shalt **keep(8104)** them, O Lord, thou shalt preserve them from this generation for ever.

Psalms 119:66-67

Teach me good judgment and knowledge: for I have believed thy commandments.
Before I was afflicted I went astray: but now have I **kept(8104)** thy word.

Psalms 119:101

I have refrained my feet from every evil way, that I might **keep(8104)** thy word.

Ecclesiastes 12:13

Let us hear the conclusion of the whole matter: Fear God, and **keep(8104)** his commandments: for this is the whole duty of man.

John 17:6

I have manifested thy name unto the men which thou gavest me out of the world: thine they were, and thou gavest them me; and they have **kept(5083)** thy word.

Mark 7:6-9

He answered and said unto them, Well hath Esaias prophesied of you hypocrites, as it is written, This people honoureth me with their lips, but their heart is far from me.
Howbeit in vain do they worship me, teaching for doctrines the commandments of men.
For laying aside the commandment of God, ye **hold(Strong's #2902, Krateo; use strength; seize or retain)** the tradition of men, as the washing of pots and cups: and many other such like things ye do.
And he said unto them, Full well ye reject the commandment of God, that ye may **keep(5083)** your own tradition.

John 14:23-24

Jesus answered and said unto him, If a man love me, he will **keep(5083)** my words: and my Father will love him, and we will come unto him, and make our abode with him.
He that loveth me not **keepeth(5083)** not my sayings: and the word which ye hear is not mine, but the Father's which sent me.

1 John 5:2-3

By this we know that we love the children of God, when we love God, and **keep(5083)** his commandments.
For this is the love of God, that we **keep(5083)** his commandments: and his commandments are not grievous.

1 Timothy 4:7

I have fought a good fight, I have finished my course, I have **kept(5083)** the faith:

Psalms 68:11

The Lord gave the word: great was the company of those that published it.

Psalms 119:16

I will delight myself in thy statutes: I will not forget thy word.

Psalms 119:105

Thy word is a lamp unto my feet, and a light unto my path.

Psalms 119:140

Thy word is very pure: therefore thy servant loveth it.

Psalm 119:11

Thy word have I hid in mine heart, that I might not sin against thee.

Psalms 119:46

I will speak of thy testimonies also before kings, and will not be ashamed.

Psalms 119:42

So shall I have wherewith to answer him that reproacheth me: for I trust in thy word.

Proverbs 2:1-11

My son, if thou wilt receive my words, and hide my commandments with thee;

So that thou incline thine ear unto wisdom, and apply thine heart to understanding;

Yea, if thou criest after knowledge, and liftest up thy voice for understanding;

If thou seekest her as silver, and searchest for her as for hid treasures;

Then shalt thou understand the fear of the Lord, and find the knowledge of God.

For the Lord giveth wisdom: out of his mouth cometh knowledge and understanding.

He layeth up sound wisdom for the righteous: he is a buckler to them that walk uprightly.

He keepeth the paths of judgment, and preserveth the way of his saints.

Then shalt thou understand righteousness, and judgment, and equity; yea, every good path. When wisdom entereth into thine heart, and knowledge is pleasant unto thy soul;

Discretion shall preserve thee, understanding shall keep thee:

CPSIA information can be obtained at www.ICGtesting.com
Printed in the USA
LVOW10s2124010715

444686LV00001B/63/P